WARNING

This book contains sexually explicit scenes and adult language. It may be considered offensive to some readers. This book is for sale to adults ONLY.

* * * * * * * * * * * * * * * *

Please store your files wisely where they cannot be accessed by underage readers.

Other books by Shyla Starr:

Tenacious Billionaire BWWM Romance Series

Adalia is too proud to accept help from the billionaire playboy, Trent Dawson. How long can she maintain her resolve? The bank is at her heels to repossess her business. To make matters worse, Adalia finds suspicious evidence of Trent's philandering ways. She must determine whether to trust Trent with the fate of her business and her heart.

Elusive Billionaire Romance Series

Billionaire Hendrick is trying to repair his company's image by putting in some volunteer work, building a school and hospital for the impoverished children in Africa. There, he meets a beautiful African American volunteer, Jocelyn. They hit it off right away but does she belong in his world?

Lonely Billionaire Romance Series

Tricia was hired to care for billionaire John's wife, who is dying. An unlikely romance emerges after his wife, Rebecca, gives John permission to pursue his happiness after she is gone.

Ardent Billionaire Romance Series

Deirdre doesn't know what to make of the gorgeous man that seems to be interested in her. His name is Parker Walters and he seems friendly enough. There is just something off about him. Why is he trying the hide the fact that he is the heir to his father's billion dollar software empire?

Fervent Billionaire BWWM Romance Series

Alexandra had never been with a white man before. She had seen William at the café before but she always kept her distance. It was unfortunate that their first chance meeting happened when she dropped her breakfast and spilled coffee all over his expensive business suit.

Audacious Billionaire BWWM Romance Series

Chante is torn between staying close to a man beyond her league, and fleeing from him to spare herself from a hopeless position. But she finds she is propelled into a place where she needs to confront her doubts and cast her fate aside to follow the dictates of her heart. Damned if she does and miserable is she doesn't, how will Chante face the events that will lead her to a place of pure happiness or to the pits of a broken heart?

Get the latest update on new releases from the author at:

https://shylastarr.com/newsletter/

This book is Part Five of the "Persuasive Billionaire BWWM Romance Series"

1 - Love Invested

Stacey is trying to keep a handle on her life the best that she can. She is on the verge of losing her job and her apartment, while taking care of her sick grandmother. Her life takes an unexpected turn when she meets Charlie, who works for the construction company that is attempting to persuade her to move out of her home.

2 - Love Divested

After discovering that Charlie has a fiancée, Stacey's world has turned upside down. She cannot help but feel as if she is in over her head. Struggling with her job, her bills and her family, will Stacey be able to figure out how she can get her life straightened out?

3 - Love Reinstated

Stacey decides that she has to put Charlie behind her and move on with her life. As Stacey dates Tony and is pulled into his world, she slowly realizes that although she likes him, it might not be enough to brush aside her feelings for Charlie. Leaving everything behind, she lets herself get lost in the money and privacy that Tony brings to her.

4 - Love Confirmed

Stacey can't believe the turn of events in her life. After losing her grandmother and running away to Tony's private island, she was content to stick her head in the sand and forget her past. But a proposal from Charlie changes everything.

5 - Love Divine

Stacey must ensure she relaxes in order to keep her baby safe. But life is never that easy. Her new husband's father is bent on sabotaging their fledgling investment firm. To make things worse, her brother-in-law isn't content with just being in the background. Stacey finds herself wishing she could have the brothers patch things up.

Persuasive Billionaire BWWM Romance Series

Love Divine

Book Five

By Shyla Starr

Table of Contents

Chapter One

"**WALK SLOWLY**. Maybe you should wait here. I can get a wheelchair."

"From where?" Stacey asked. "I'm fine, really."

Charlie frowned and reached out for her anyway. He slid his arm around her waist to help her walk into the lobby of their apartment complex. Stacey knew that she could walk fine without his help but didn't want to shrug him off.

She had spent the night in the hospital. There were those terrifying moments that Stacey had been utterly convinced something dreadful had happened to the baby. She felt sore all over as if a train hit her.

But the doctor said the baby was okay. She was a high-risk pregnancy and would have to take things slowly. He told her to cut back on work and stress. Stacey couldn't help but think of Charlie and his family, her new job with William, and Charlie's own investment firm starting up. Cut back on stress. How in the world was she going to do that?

There was no time to talk to Charlie about what his brother, Eric, had told her. Eric warned her that their father, Terry, was going to move against Charlie. At the time, Stacey decided not to tell Charlie because she didn't want to upset him. Now that Eric had drunkenly blathered about it, she saw it in a new light. Charlie perceived it as Stacey keeping a secret from him, something she only shared with Eric, his brother, of all people.

As they made their way up to the penthouse, she wondered how she should apologize and try to make what happened clear to him. Charlie, who became incredibly drunk last night, was now extremely hungover. His skin was sick looking, with a slight yellow tinge to it. His hair was messy and he still wore the same clothes from the other night. He was now drinking water and coffee non-stop. Both of them needed a nap.

At home, Charlie led her directly to bed. Stacey sunk into the massive bed gratefully, pulling the sheets over her. She knew that she needed to talk to him about Eric and what he had said, but she suddenly felt more exhausted than ever. Everything that had happened seemed to sweep over her all at once and she felt as if she had emotional whiplash.

"Charlie…" she mumbled as he crawled into bed next to her.

"It's okay," he whispered back and brought her close against him.

Stacey could hear the steady beat of his heart. Her eyelids closed without effort. All her limbs felt as if they each weighed a thousand pounds. Before she could utter another word, she fell fast asleep.

<<<>>>

In her dream, there was a baby crying in the distance. Stacey knew that this was hers. She was in Tina's old house, at the dining room table. She felt rooted to the chair as if she couldn't move. Next to her was Allison. She was ignoring her homework again, covering her page in doodles.

Stacey could hear the TV playing in the living room. Some part of her realized this was the night she found out about her parents' deaths. The baby cried louder in the distance.

Fighting against the pull that was keeping her to her chair, she managed to stand up. Allison didn't glance at her – it was as if Stacey wasn't even there. Stacey felt hot all over, as though she suddenly came down with a fever.

The phone rang. She knew what the news was going to be. Quickly, she darted out of the dining room. If she kept running, she wouldn't have to hear the news. She just had to keep moving.

She ran to the front door and yanked it open. Behind her, Tina was letting out a wailing cry. Stacey stepped outside and slammed the door shut. The front yard was covered in a thick layer of snow. The moon was covered by clouds and almost everything was dark.

She cut across the yard. The crying got louder now. She could see a cradle in the distance. She hurried, anxious to get to it.

But as Stacey approached the cradle, a sharp pain shot through her body. It felt like she was getting stabbed. Her knees weakened and she hit the ground. The snow around her turned red. She let out a gasp.

"You're okay! You're okay, Stacey. It was just a dream."

Stacey's eyes opened and she found herself staring up at Charlie. His arms were wrapped firmly around her, and he was clutching her close to his chest. Her breathing was coming hard and fast as if she just ran a mile. She could still see the snow around her, turning dark with her own blood as her baby in the cradle cried.

She shivered and said, "I'm okay. Sorry. Did I wake you up?"

"Yeah. You were making a whimpering noise." He pushed back a strand of hair that fell in front of her eyes. "You sounded terrified."

Stacey's mouth felt dry, as if it was stuffed full of cotton. The room was dark except for the hallway light shining through the crack in the door. They must have forgotten to shut it off when they got home.

"What time is it?" she asked.

"Little after three in the morning."

"And I woke you up. I'm sorry," she said again.

"Hey, it's okay. Really. Do you want to talk about the dream?"

Stacey thought about Tina answering that phone call that changed everything. The thought of her parents and Tina, now all gone, made her heart ache. She silently shook her head. Charlie nodded and then got out of bed.

"Need some water. Want some?"

"Yes, please."

She watched him go and tried to calm down her racing heart. She told herself it was just a dream. She had weird dreams all the time. This one was no different. How could she not have crazy dreams after what she just went through?

Stacey sat up and brought the blanket around her. It was slightly chilly in the room. She reached over to check her phone. There were two missed calls from Allison, who left shortly before Stacey was discharged from the hospital. She left only because Jacob's father recently fell and had been sent to a hospital out of state. Stacey ordered her sister to leave, telling her over and over again that she was fine and so was the baby. Stacey felt it was important for Allison to be with Jacob.

She made a mental note to call Allison first thing to try to calm her nerves. She could picture her sister right now, nervously pacing the hotel room, torn between her and Jacob.

Charlie came back with two glasses of water and handed one to her. Then he sat down next to her and took a swig from his glass. Stacey mumbled a thank you and drank half of her water in one gulp. She was incredibly thirsty for some reason.

"I shouldn't have stormed out of the party like that," he finally said.

Out of everything for him to say, Stacey was surprised by this. She wasn't even thinking about how he hadn't been there right at the start of things. She was too busy trying to form an apology in her head.

"You don't have to be sorry," she replied.

"Yeah, I do. If I'd stayed – if I'd stayed even a minute longer…" he trailed off.

Stacey grabbed his hand, shaking her head. "No, Charlie. It wouldn't have changed anything."

"If I hadn't gotten angry with you over what Eric said. Being drunk isn't an excuse. I should have stopped myself and discussed it with you. Instead, I got angry and you ended up in the hospital."

"One has nothing to do with the other," she said firmly.

But Charlie shrugged and looked morosely at his glass before saying, "Maybe not."

"They don't. And even if you were there, nothing would have changed. Eric found you a minute later, didn't he?"

"I know. I know it's pointless to beat myself up over it. I was terrified that you were hurt or something happened to the baby."

"Well, I'm okay. I just need to relax."

"You're so good at that," he joked and smiled at her.

"Well, just keep me in check." She poked his abs playfully and smiled back.

Charlie leaned over and kissed her gently before saying, "I'm sorry that I got angry. I'm basically sorry for the entire night. Made me remember why I don't drink like that."

"No, I'm sorry for not telling you about what Eric warned me about."

She hesitated for a moment and then decided to tell him the entire thing. She told him of how Eric had warned her about Terry not being pleased back in the hallway at the manor. She admitted to slapping him and feeling ashamed at having done so. Stacey then finished with Eric telling her that his becoming president was bullshit and wouldn't happen.

Charlie leaned back in bed. "I knew there must have been a reason why Eric wasn't taking things seriously. I mean, don't get me wrong. He never takes things seriously. But this was different. This was something he had been saying for years he deserved. It lands in his lap yet he doesn't want it? It didn't make sense."

"What are you going to do about your father?"

He shrugged. "Ignore him."

"No, Charlie, I'm serious."

"So am I."

Stacey shook her head. "Eric seems to be taking this really seriously. When he mentioned it in the hallway, I just assumed he was trying to start things and that you knew already what Terry was up to. But you don't. You could lose this entire business before it even gets off the ground."

"Stacey, do not worry about it. Please. It isn't going to help you at all to fret about it. Eric warned you, but I know now. I'll figure it out."

"I don't get why he didn't just go to you in the first place."

Charlie laughed at that. "Really? I do. He wanted to help me out but didn't want to come to me directly. Easier to go through you."

"I just thought…"

"Thought what?"

"Well, sometimes you seemed upset that Eric was speaking to me. So, I thought he told me this just to piss you off. As if he and I were close," she said this all quickly, as if she was yanking off a bandage that had been on for too long.

There was a small intake of breath from Charlie. For a second, Stacey was worried that she pissed him off. He was touchy when it came to Eric, who seemed to know every nerve to press against his older brother.

"Jealous. Maybe a little," he admitted.

"Why in the world? No offense but your brother is maddening, to say the least."

He chuckled. "Tell me about it. I don't know. I guess it's because I knew what he was doing. He was buddy-buddy with you. I've had it happen before where –" He cut himself off as if he was saying too much.

But Stacey pressed, "What? Had what happen before?"

As if remembering their last fight about him keeping things close to his chest, Charlie said quickly, "Him flirting with past girlfriends before. And I've had them… go for it."

Stacey was aghast, "What? How?"

"He's funny and charming. You've seen him. He enters a room like he owns it."

"So do you," she countered.

But Charlie shook his head. "No, Eric is different. He's cocky. He's got this sort of swagger to him that some women just eat up. Including some ex-girlfriends."

"So, what, exactly? You thought I'd be tempted?" Stacey asked, aghast.

"No! No, no, this is coming out wrong. There was no way I thought you'd ever make a move on Eric. But I didn't trust him with you. I could just picture him, feeding you all these little secrets or stupid notions. Suggesting I wasn't on your side. I didn't think he'd swoop in and kiss you or anything. No, I thought he'd just keep stirring the pot. Making you think I wasn't on your side when it came to my dad."

"So… when he told you that he warned me about Terry…"

"Drunken me just sort of panicked. I took that as a sign you two were getting close. That whatever Eric was scheming was working." He looked at her seriously. "I'm sober now though. I know that isn't the case. I know that I overreacted. I just…"

"What?"

"I just don't trust Eric with you."

"I know he's a cocky bastard, but I saw you two drunk together. You were laughing and having fun. Surely, somewhere deep down you two want to be like that all the time."

Charlie didn't reply. He shrugged a little and avoided looking at her.

But Stacey didn't want to drop it just yet. "You two are still brothers. There is still a connection there, somewhere. It's just gotten mangled up with everything going on."

"Stacey, I know what you're trying to do. And I appreciate it. Really, I do. But Eric and I aren't going to be like you and Allison. There isn't any understanding to be found between us. There's too much bad blood. And frankly, being around him this much lately has reminded me why we don't just casually hang out."

"I guess," she mumbled although she still wasn't convinced.

Charlie leaned over to her and kissed the top of her head, "Don't worry about me and Eric. I'm used to how we are. It's just how it has to be. We should try to sleep now."

She nodded and Charlie tucked her into bed. He curled up next to her. Stacey could feel the warmth from his body. Before she could say anything else, he was already snoring.

Yet Stacey couldn't fall asleep right off the bat. Her mind was swirling with all sorts of different things. She was worried about the baby. She was worried about work and Charlie. And even though he said there was no reconciliation with Eric, she wasn't yet convinced.

She focused on her breathing. It took a little while but eventually Stacey drifted back to sleep.

Chapter Two

"I'm okay. I promise. How is Jacob?"

"Alright. Actually," Allison lowered her voice, "it all feels weird. Like, we're all just waiting around for his dad to pass on. Maybe it's a rich person thing."

Stacey snorted, "I doubt it."

"Well, in any case, I'm just sitting here like we're on death watch. He's been sick for months, so no one is too surprised or anything. Jacob is pretty quiet. Honestly, I wish I was there with you."

"I'm fine, really."

"The doctor said no stress and to relax. You're shitty at both of those things," Allison replied.

"I'm a quick learner."

"Well, as soon as I get back into town, I'm keeping an eye on you. Strict bed rest. Going to corner William and make sure he doesn't keep you overworked."

"William was really sweet about the whole thing. Said I could work from home."

"You shouldn't be working at all."

"I'm not going to sit around and do nothing all day," Stacey replied, "so don't start."

She heard her sister sigh before saying, "We'll discuss it later. Keep me posted, okay?"

With the call over, Stacey leaned back against the couch. Charlie had gone into the office even though he hadn't wanted to. But Stacey didn't want to keep him. She was sure that whatever his father was planning was already underway.

Daytime television hadn't improved since the last time Stacey watched it. Charlie had every channel under the sun; the kind of selection that would have left Tina dizzy with options. However, Stacey ended up watching one of those terrible day time court room shows.

She was feeling restless - it snuck up on her. The thought of spending every day like this annoyed her. She was used to being on the go. For her entire life, Stacey worked as hard as possible. She put long hours in at William's diner. She worked at Tony's with the goal of achieving more. She was on the path she wanted until she lost her way with Tony.

Now, the idea of sitting around and letting life pass her by because she was on bed rest left a bad taste in her mouth. Her laptop was in the other room. She was going to check her e-mails at least.

She had just gotten up when the elevator made a soft noise and someone stepped in.

"Charlie," she sighed, "I'm fine. I told you. I can handle it."

"I'll let him know."

Eric came into the living room. He was awkwardly holding a vase of flowers and stood in the doorway. Stacey was surprised to see him. She hadn't seen him since the night in the bathroom.

"Eric, hey. What are you doing here?"

"Uh, these are for you. 'Get well' flowers. Or… 'Glad you're well' flowers? I don't know." He held them out at her and looked like a child holding out a test with a good grade on it.

Stacey took the vase from him gingerly. Eric ran his hands through his hair and looked away from her. The vase was brimming with freshly cut flowers, all vividly colored and beautiful to look at.

"Wow, thanks. You didn't have to do this," she replied.

"I did. I was a dick the other night."

"Just the other night?"

He looked abashed. "Well, I can't give you flowers for *all* the times I was a dick. I'd be giving you flowers all day and Charlie might get angry."

"You weren't that bad the other night. Just drunk."

"I wasn't *that* drunk, Stace. I remember you being furious with me."

It was true. She had flipped out on him, furious that he went to Charlie and babbled about their father. In hindsight, she should have kept her cool. Eric was drunk and wasn't thinking clearly.

She shrugged. "It's fine now." She turned around to go put the flowers on the coffee table.

Eric trailed after her. "You and Charlie talked?"

"Yeah. We're fine. We worked it out." She skipped the details of how Charlie didn't trust Eric or the fact she knew he slept with his ex-girlfriends.

"Great. Good." He shoved his hands into his pockets.

She frowned. "What's wrong with you?"

"Nothing. Nothing new, anyway. I just – it was scary, you know? You ending up in the hospital. I just wanted to make sure you were okay."

Stacey sat back down on the couch. "I'm fine. Thanks for checking in."

Before Eric could say anything, the elevator doors opened. This time it had to be Charlie. Eric straightened and took his hands out of his pockets. Any sort of vulnerability he was showing in giving her the flowers was quickly erased.

Charlie hurried in and stopped when he saw Eric. "Uh. Hi."

"Hey," Eric said stiffly.

Her mind flickered back to the two of them drunkenly laughing and she stood up. "Eric brought me get well flowers."

Charlie narrowed his eyes. "How kind of him."

Stacey held back a sigh and stared at Charlie directly. She was going to have these two get along. She just had to keep at it.

Something in her glare must have struck Charlie because he turned to Eric and said, "Nice of you."

Eric looked disarmed for a moment before mumbling a 'no problem.' Stacey took control of the conversation.

"You're home early."

"I wanted to make sure you were doing alright. And…" He hesitated and glanced over at Eric. "Weren't you supposed to be at the office?"

"Was I?"

"Yes," Charlie said, clearly trying not to lose his patience. "Stacey, can I speak to you in private?"

"Yeah, sure," she replied, confused.

She followed Charlie down to his office where the two brothers had been recently bickering. He closed the door behind her and sat down in one of the chairs. For the first time since he got home, Stacey got a good look at him. He looked deflated, as if someone had sapped all the energy out of him.

"What's wrong?" she asked, sitting in the chair next to him.

"I don't want to stress you out, but whatever Eric warned us about… it's already happening. I lost two investors today."

"Already? I thought things were going smoothly."

"Yeah. Probably too smoothly, now that I think about it. You know last night, how you mentioned I should talk to Terry?"

"Yeah."

"Well, I think I'm going to."

"What are you going to tell him?"

"I don't know yet. Something. I have to make him stop this stupid shit. What sort of father does this? Complains about how his son runs things and then tries to botch the son's plan to branch out?"

"Someone very controlling, I would imagine."

"Well, I'm going to head up to the manor tomorrow. I know Allison is out of town, but I could get –"

"Whoa, whoa. Wait. You think you're going to confront your father and leave me at home?" Stacey asked.

Charlie blinked. "You can't come with me. The doctor said no stress."

"It isn't me confronting my father. It's you," she replied.

"Even so! Last time we went to see my father, we fought. A lot. And you slapped Eric. Which is amazing, don't get me wrong. But it was stressful."

"I want to be there to support you. You're going to need someone on your side, maybe even to back you up, if need be. Also, I know what to expect this time. I can handle myself," she protested.

Charlie sighed. There was a knock at the door.

"What?!" he snapped.

Eric opened the door and leaned into the room. "Couldn't help but overhear."

"Really?" Charlie drawled.

"You're gonna tell off Dad? You think that'll work?"

"What's your fantastic idea then?"

Eric strolled into the room and leaned against one of the bookshelves. He looked almost thoughtful, "Definitely wouldn't go with that. I mean, Dad won't care what you say. Nothing will change his mind. He wants you back in control of the company. It's just a pride thing. Come on, Charlie. Even you have to know how he gets."

"Yeah, but this is stupid. Even for him," Charlie replied.

"Doesn't matter what we think either way. Dad wants you in charge. Not me."

"Why not you? Why does it matter? I mean, Charlie is leaving but the company will still be in the family," Stacey said.

Charlie didn't answer. Eric's mouth twisted for a moment before he mumbled something she didn't make out.

"What?"

"I said because Charlie was groomed for this sort of thing. Not me," Eric said loudly. "In any case, Dad won't care if you want him to stop. You could ask him a thousand times and he won't care. But I'll come with you anyway."

"Why? I don't want you there," said Charlie sternly.

"Maybe we both can team up."

"Yeah. Maybe," Charlie replied, suddenly looking thoughtful.

Stacey could see by the way the two brothers stared at each other that neither one of them was completely sold on the idea of teaming up against Terry.

Chapter Three

The manor didn't seem to be nearly as scary as the last time Stacey was there. Perhaps it was because she had given up hope of impressing Terry. She cared more about remaining relaxed and supporting Charlie than caring what Terry thought of her. She rubbed her belly absently as the manor came into sight.

Next to her, Charlie was gripping the steering wheel of the rental car. His knuckles turned white from the force of it. She reached out and touched his shoulder. He glanced at her out of the corner of his eye before looking back at the road.

"I'm fine," he said.

Behind them came a snort followed by, "Yeah, right. The way you're sitting is enough to give you a back ache."

Stacey glanced at Eric. He was taking up the entire backseat as if it were a bed. He had his phone in his hands and had been texting with someone ever since they landed. Probably a woman, she thought as he looked up at her.

"Relaxing?" she asked him.

"No point in stressing out about trying to talk to Dad."

"If you think it won't work then why are you here?" she asked him.

Eric ignored the question and instead directed one toward Charlie, "I know it's a rental, but I'll blow the smoke out the window."

"No," Charlie replied firmly.

Variations of this conversation had unfolded since they had piled into the rental car. Eric rolled his eyes and fiddled with the cigarette pack he was holding in his lap as if just being near it helped him relax.

"I'm just going to chain smoke like, this entire pack once we get there."

"I don't care if you eat them. The rental car is non-smoking."

"Well, good for the car that it doesn't smoke but I, unfortunately, am not non-smoking," Eric quipped.

"Seriously, why are you here?" Stacey pressed with her question. "If you think Terry won't budge on this thing."

Eric looked at her for a long moment and then finally said, "Well, Charlie and I have never teamed up to try to talk to him before."

"It isn't teaming up," Charlie snapped. "We're just going to be in the same room."

"Talking to him about the same stuff and trying to make him not sound like an asshole," Eric replied swiftly, "I would consider that to be on the same side."

Charlie was about to say something no doubt unhelpful when Stacey said, "Can you two not fight about if you're on the same side about a fight? Honestly. Charlie."

"Not just me," he mumbled as if he were a five-year-old.

"Not just me either," Eric shot back.

Stacey threw her hands up in the air. "You two – *both of you,* might I add – are acting ridiculous. Charlie, your father is literally trying to ruin your investment firm before it takes off, and you're too busy debating semantics with Eric instead of being glad he is here."

Charlie fell silent. A smug look crossed Eric's face but Stacey turned to look at him.

"And you shouldn't be focused on bothering Charlie. This affects you too, doesn't it? Stop treating everything like a joke and be a little more active in what's going on."

Eric's lips pressed firmly together but he didn't say anything. The car filled with silence for the first time since they had gotten into it. Stacey turned and leaned back in her seat.

"If you both really want to talk to Terry, you have to put up a united front. He'll try to get you two to fight with each other instead of him."

"And how do you know that?" Eric drawled from behind.

"Makes sense, doesn't it? He knows you two don't get along. He won't take you guys seriously until you show him you mean business."

The car fell silent again. Stacey pulled out a thin paperback book she had brought with her and began to read, signaling the end of the conversation. Both Charlie and Eric were mercifully quiet.

It was funny, Stacey thought, how much the two brothers didn't get along. The more she watched them interact and the more she learned about Terry, the more Stacey became convinced it was nothing more than the fact the two of them were pitted against each other since their mother died.

Maybe it was a fool's errand, but Stacey was still convinced that the two of them could mend the broken bridge between them and become close again.

By the time they pulled up to the manor, snow had begun to fall. It was the first time that Stacey saw snow since winter officially began. She pulled her coat around her tightly as they got out of the car.

"We aren't welcome," Eric pointed out when no one came out to greet them.

"That's not new for me," Stacey joked although Charlie frowned in response.

"Come on," he said.

Stacey and Eric followed him to the large front doors. The manor looked even more dark and foreboding with the winter sky behind it. Next to her, Eric slid a cigarette out and lit it up.

"I thought you were trying to hide that from him."

"What's the point now?" Eric replied as he took a long drag off of it and sighed in pleasure. "He's going to be furious with us soon anyway. This way I can just slide the smoking part in so it gets lumped with everything else."

He puffed out a smoke circle and watched it warp and twist up into the sky. Charlie pulled a key out of his coat pocket and shoved it in the lock. It turned and opened with a click. He yanked the door open and looked behind him.

"Come on. And Eric, hurry up. We don't have time to sit around so you can smoke."

"One more puff," he replied quickly.

Stacey followed Charlie into the hallway. The manor was as silent as a tomb. Eric hurried in after them, reeking of cigarette smoke. Peter didn't magically appear to greet them. Stacey glanced at Charlie who looked as if he was wavering.

"Maybe he isn't here," he said to her.

"No, he's here," Eric replied. "Where would he go? No one likes him, remember."

Charlie grabbed Stacey's hand. Even though it was cold outside, his hand was warm from his nerves. Eric made a noise that she couldn't make out. The three of them headed toward the living room.

"Hear that?" Eric mumbled.

She did. Voices. She relaxed slightly. At least someone was here. She was starting to wonder if Terry went somewhere and hadn't bothered to tell them. Showing up here would have been for nothing.

They entered the living room. Charlie stopped abruptly which caused Stacey to run into his back. Eric reached out and steadied her. His hand was warm like Charlie's. He must have been just as nervous as Charlie was.

"What is this?"

Stacey moved so she could see into the living room. It was Charlie who spoke and when she looked in the room she could see why.

Terry was sitting on the couch with Peter standing behind him. On a chair across from Terry sat, of all people, Adele.

Stacey hadn't seen her since the night Charlie proposed. She had cut her hair. It was angled to frame her face perfectly. Her eyes looked wide and luminous. A slow smile spread across her face when she saw the three of them. She looked like a cat that had just cornered a mouse.

"Charlie. Eric. So nice to see you," Adele said, crossing her legs to show them off.

Charlie ignored her and turned to Terry, "We have to speak to you."

"As you can see, I'm busy," his father replied and then looked over at Eric. "Why are you here, boy?"

"He said 'we,' Dad. Not just him. *We* have to speak to you," Eric replied.

Terry scoffed, "Go wait outside for me. Peter will show you to one of the sitting rooms."

"No," Charlie replied and crossed his arms.

"Eric, take your brother and his.... wife," he lingered on the word as if it left a dirty taste in his mouth, "and go sit in one of the other rooms."

"No, we're fine here. Besides, you shouldn't be alone with Adele. I heard the way she unhinges her jaw in order to engulf an entire man is a mighty sight to behold but ultimately deadly," said Charlie, keeping a straight face.

Stacey stifled a laugh and avoided looking at Adele. Terry's jaw set. His eyes jumped from the brothers to her. No doubt he was getting ready to blame her for the brothers standing against him. Even so, she felt oddly calm. It was as if she was watching the events unfold through a window.

"Oh, let them stay," Adele spoke up, leaning back in the chair. "No harm in it."

"I know what you're doing. With the investment firm and getting my backers to jump ship. Whatever else you have up your sleeve, I want you to stop it. This is my business, not yours. Put Eric in control of the company and leave me out of it. I told you I was leaving. I need you to respect that, Father." Charlie spoke quickly and looked slightly sick but kept going, "I need you to respect that I'm going out on my own. I don't understand what the issue is. You hated not being in control of the company when you got too ill."

Then Eric spoke, "Also, I don't want to be in charge of it either. Not like this, anyway. You know, I've been thinking a lot about how much you spoke about the company after Mom died. You groomed Charlie to run it so why do I want the stupid thing so badly? I've come to the conclusion that you *wanted* me to want it. Speaking soft words here and there as if Charlie stole something from me. But he didn't take anything from me. I just thought he did. So take the company and find someone else to run it because I don't want it," and then he added, almost as an afterthought, "and, by the way, I'm a smoker. So there."

Terry didn't reply. He looked carefully at Charlie and then at Eric. The two of them were silent.

Then Terry laughed. Stacey was startled. It was the first time she had heard him laugh like that. It wasn't a nice laugh. It sounded hoarse, like sandpaper being dragged across glass. She flinched as if she had been struck.

"I see what is going on here," Terry finally said after laughing. "You two idiots think you can come in here and tell me what's going to happen. Did *she* put that into your heads?" He jerked his head toward Stacey.

"This isn't about me. This is about you," Stacey replied calmly.

A flicker of surprise crossed Terry's face as if he couldn't believe she actually had the nerve to speak to him. But Stacey realized she wasn't afraid of him. He was a bully, wasn't he? He bullied his own sons and used them against each other. Her parents always loved her. Tina always loved her. She was lucky enough to have a family that cared about her. Terry let his heart die with his wife. She pitied him.

"I don't want you meddling any more in my life or in what I'm doing. Stacey is pregnant, Dad. And if you act like this, you won't see my child because I wouldn't want the baby around you."

Stacey looked over at Charlie in surprise. He never mentioned this to her. He glanced at her nervously but she only nodded slightly in agreement.

"And I just want you to leave me alone too," Eric said. "I'm sick of being your errand boy."

Terry turned his gaze to Eric. The expression on his face was openly hostile. There was something raw about it that unsettled Stacey. For some reason, she felt as if she had to throw herself over Eric to protect him from whatever his father was about to unleash.

"Leave you alone? To do what, exactly? You have amounted to exactly nothing, boy. Now that you can finally do something, you back down. You don't want to control the company. You don't want to help out your brother. You don't want to help me out anymore. What if I cut you out of the will and left you with nothing? What would you do?" he snorted. "Absolutely nothing, I bet! Because you *are* nothing. It's this family name that gives you any worth and you're trying to toss that aside. Do it then. Rot for all I care. You haven't proven yourself to be good at anything besides dirtying yourself with low class women and slacking off."

Eric's chest was rising and falling rapidly. Stacey felt a flash of anger shoot through her after Terry finished speaking. The expression on Eric's face was something she had never seen before. The mask of arrogance he usually wore was now yanked away. He suddenly didn't look like a grown man but a child being scolded. His bottom lip quivered and for one terrible moment she wondered if Eric was going to cry. She didn't think she could stand it if he did. It seemed so unlike him.

Before Eric could say anything in response, Terry swung his gaze to Charlie. "And you, boy. You have been groomed for this since you were young. It's true. I didn't want to give you the company. Often I feel as if you make stupid choices and are blundering through things. That business with the city renovation, for one thing. Losing that entire profit for a woman." His face contorted into a sneer as his gaze shot over to Stacey for a moment. "Stupidity through and through. And now you want to leave – after everything I've done for you? I have supported you through the good and bad. You want to embarrass me and make me look like a fool. It's a matter of pride, Charlie. I am doing this so that you can see what mistakes you're making. Your firm will never take off because I won't allow it. Come back to the company before I have to ruin you completely."

Charlie went completely still. He looked as if he was carved out of marble. Stacey didn't dare look at Eric. She couldn't imagine what he looked like right now. Terry's speech to Charlie was kinder although that wasn't saying much. She hadn't considered Terry to have favorites before today. Now it was clear that he preferred Charlie.

He still didn't reply. Terry took this as a sign to keep going, as if sensing it as an advantage. "I only did what I did because I am trying to have you see how foolish this all is. You want to leave the company you were made for. I only ever objected to things you did to help you learn. When I die, this company is yours, Charlie. I can't allow you to give up being president to run off on this folly."

"You're right," Charlie finally said.

Behind her, Eric called his brother something terrible. Stacey felt shocked herself and turned to look at him. She was about to ask him how he could agree with his father when Charlie kept going.

"I mean, you're not right about this. You're right about something you told me when I was thirteen. I broke some stupid vase accidentally when Eric and I were playing a game. Smashed it to pieces. I remember you looming over me, larger than life, telling me that once you ruin something like that, it can't be fixed. I could spend hours gluing the pieces together and you'd see the cracks all over it."

Terry didn't say anything.

"And you're right. Once something is broken like that, those cracks are there. In vases and in humans. And frankly, I'm sick of patching up all the cracks from your insanity and your stupid lessons. So, if you want to crush your own son's business, go ahead. But I'm not coming back to control the company, no matter what you do."

Terry's face darkened to an ugly shade of red. Stacey was glad he was so feeble; otherwise, she could see him lunging at Charlie.

"You're an idiot. Just like your brother. No different," he finally hissed at Charlie.

Next to her, Eric sucked in a small breath as if he was being physically wounded. Stacey wanted to reach out for him but she knew he'd shrug her off.

"Fine," their father said. "If that is how you want things done, then so be it. I'll go on with my own plan."

"And you're going to tell us what it is now, aren't you?" Eric finally spoke up. "As if you're going to really prove us wrong."

"Found your voice again, did you?" Terry sneered at Eric who balked. "I don't need you posing as president anymore. I'm marrying Adele."

Both Charlie and Eric exclaimed in surprise. Stacey wrinkled her nose. Terry looked ancient. Adele sat in the chair, looking smugly at them.

"What the hell is wrong with you?" It was Eric who spoke first. "That's disgusting. She's young enough to be your daughter."

"Adele's family and I will merge our companies through the agreement that she gets by marrying into our family. Since neither of you two morons will take it, once again I have to step up."

"Step up, really? To fucking someone that young? Wow, Dad, you're so brave. Mom would be so fucking proud of you," Eric spat angrily and then turned around, storming out of the living room.

Charlie watched him go and then looked with disgust at his father. He didn't say anything else. Instead, he grabbed Stacey's hand and pulled her out of the living room. He was yanking her down the hallway now. She allowed herself to be pulled along until they went into one of the small sitting rooms. Charlie shut the door behind them and ran his fingers through his hair.

Eric must have followed them because they didn't even get a chance to speak before the door bursted back open.

"Let's go. Come on. Book a flight or whatever," he gestured to Charlie.

"I'm not leaving yet," Charlie replied, "I'm just cooling off."

"What?" He got close to him. "Why aren't you leaving? There isn't anything left to do here."

"I have to talk Dad out of this, okay? He can't marry Adele. That's insanity."

"Who cares? It isn't our business what that crazy old man decides to do!" Eric yelled. "If he wants to marry that witch and merge with them, let him! Why do you care?"

"Mom wouldn't want this."

"Mom is dead!" Eric shouted so loudly that Charlie took a step back. "She's dead. She won't care what Dad does or doesn't do. She isn't going to come down from Heaven to bless us if we stop him from making irrational life choices!"

"He's still family, Eric! He's still our dad."

"No." He was backing up now as if he had been slapped, shaking his head. "No. He's nothing. He's not a fucking thing."

He threw one look at Stacey and then stormed out of the sitting room, slamming the door shut behind him so hard that the wall rattled.

Chapter Four

"Maybe we should go," Stacey said very softly after Eric stormed out.

Charlie threw himself down onto the nearest chair. The sitting room was full of bookshelves filled with books that gave off a slight musty scent. Dust swirled in the light from the windows. She sat down in a chair across from Charlie.

"He's going to marry Adele. I can't wrap my head around it."

"Yes. But he's a grown man. He can make his own choices."

He let out a bitter laugh. "He can make choices for everyone else. His own end up seeming questionable at best."

"I'm not trying to pick sides," Stacey said carefully, "but Eric does have a point. He hasn't treated either of you with kindness. There were no heartfelt emotions expressed in there, Charlie. Just poison spewing out of his mouth."

"He's always like that."

"That doesn't mean you and your brother should be accepting of it." When he didn't reply, she tried again. "What do you think will happen if he marries Adele?"

"He's only doing this because I'm leaving, I know that. I know he's doing it as some kind of control method. As if I'd *want* him to marry Adele. And she'll marry anyone in this family for the money. All this talk about a merger is bullshit. It's just to get under my skin. And it's working! Of course it's working. Dad, the master manipulator."

"So, call his bluff. Let him marry her."

Charlie was drumming his fingers against the arm of the chair but at this moment he stopped. "What do you mean?"

"Your dad is clearly doing an awful lot to get you to come back to the company. That means he needs you, Charlie. He needs you more than you need him. That's why he's trying so desperately to get you to come back, including this stunt with Adele. So let him marry her. I doubt he'll really go through with it."

"You don't know my dad like I do," he mumbled.

"So, if he wants to marry a snake like that, let him. I think you should just live your life the way you want and not let your dad manipulate you into coming back to the company. He's grasping at straws because you're doing what you want without his approval."

He met her gaze. His eyes softened a little and a small smile crossed his face. "You're a smart woman, Stacey."

She smiled back. "I know. Someone has to be the smart one in this relationship."

He stood up. "Let's leave. And get Eric before he punches someone in the face. Hopefully not me."

Charlie held his hand out to her. Stacey took it and stood up. His hand was firm, not as nervously warm as it previously was. He leaned over and kissed her gently on the lips. In that moment, Stacey couldn't have been more proud of him.

The trio hit a patch of bad luck trying to get a flight home. They missed the last flight back to the city, leaving them driving to the nearest town to try to find a hotel for the night.

The drive in was silent. Stacey could feel waves of anger and irritation rolling off of Eric. It felt as if it was filling the car with nothing but negativity. At one point, he pulled out a cigarette and lit it, rolling down the window to blow the smoke out. The entire time, he stared at Charlie as if challenging him about the fact he was smoking in the car. To Stacey's relief, he didn't say anything to Eric.

The nearest town to the manor was small and offered a tourist trap museum claiming to be the

World's Biggest Collection of Smallest Teapots. They drove past it on the way to the hotel.

"Wow, that place looks riveting," Stacey joked as they drove by.

She heard Charlie laugh quietly but Eric's expression remained unchanged. He was opening his pack for another cigarette but Stacey saw that it was empty. He made an irritated noise in the back of his throat and slumped against the back seat.

They stopped at a fast food place for dinner and ate quietly. A light snow covered the car as they got in to drive to the hotel.

The place looked run down. The neon sign illuminating the name of *Neptune Suites* was half burnt out. The snow was coming down heavier now, sticking to the sign and melting against the lights that were working. The hotel itself was all ground level with a tiny pool in the center that had a CLOSED sign on the gate.

"Sure you can stay here, Charlie? Might not be nice enough for you," Eric sneered.

For once, Charlie didn't reply. He seemed to sense that Eric was looking for a fight and that it was better not to go after him. They walked into the lobby where a sleepy-looking man gave them two room keys.

Eric went into his without saying a word and shut the door firmly behind him. Stacey and Charlie took the other room. It was barebones, with a bed and a small television that looked ancient. A lone painting of a beach was thrown up on one of the walls.

"It'll do. I'm exhausted," Charlie said as he tossed his bag onto the floor.

He yanked the sheets down and crawled under them, pulling the covers over. Stacey rummaged through her bag for her toothbrush. She couldn't sleep without brushing her teeth first.

Charlie mumbled something into his pillow and Stacey replied, "What?"

He pushed himself up and looked at her. "Thanks. For everything you did today. I would have stayed to try to convince Dad not to marry her. I would have fallen right into his stupid trap. But you helped me… helped give me the strength to leave."

"You were always strong enough to do that. You just needed a little push. What do you think Terry thought when you left?"

"I don't know. I don't know if he figured we'd leave and then go crawling back, or what."

"What about Eric? Terry wasn't nice to you, but he was downright cruel to your brother," Stacey said.

Disgust crossed Charlie's face. "How could he just tell his own son that he was nothing?" He rolled onto his back and sat up. "Eric and I have never gotten along but I've been thinking about what you've said. And just about me and Eric in general as we drove over here."

Stacey went over and sat down next to him on the bed. "What are you thinking?"

"Dad was always harder on Eric. Like, not in a way to help him succeed but just in an asshole sort of way. I wonder if it's because he's like our mom."

"Eric is like your mom?" Stacey asked, surprised and trying to picture Charlie's mother as a sarcastic smart ass.

"From what I remember, she was really great with people. They flocked to her. Sort of like what Eric can do in a room. Mom was funny too. She was witty and a quick thinker. Eric is too."

"So, your father takes things out on Eric because he reminds him of your mother. Makes sense but still completely wrong and terrible."

"I wonder if Dad just takes out his anger about Mom dying on Eric. It's still fucked up either way. I don't know what Eric is going to do now. We've both always wanted Dad's approval for so long. Living with that desire… neither one of us are just going to be able to shake it off, you know?"

"Your dad sounds like he thrived off manipulating his own sons. That's what he lived for. And with you about to break free and start things on your own, it sounds as if he's trying everything to keep you under his thumb," Stacey remarked.

"Yeah, it's a good plan. Dad was always good at figuring out what would drive the other person crazy. In business and with me and Eric. He knew I'd be disgusted with him marrying Adele. He has to think that I'm going to agree to come back to the business just so he doesn't marry her."

"Why do you think he said those things to Eric?" Stacey asked curiously. "Trying to marry Adele to manipulate you into coming back – I understand it even though it's insane. But he was downright cruel to him."

"I don't know. Maybe he thought full on force like that was enough to bring Eric back. He did threaten to cut him out of the will too. He probably thinks Eric wouldn't be able to function without any money. Honestly, Dad might have a point there. Eric enjoys a certain lifestyle."

Just then, Charlie yawned. Stacey leaned over and kissed him before saying, "You should get some sleep."

His eyes were already closing as he snuggled down into bed. He mumbled good-night as Stacey went over to the bathroom to brush her teeth. By the time she finished, Charlie was fast asleep, snoring quietly.

Stacey studied his face. The face of her husband. She still wasn't used to that word. So much had happened lately. Everything felt as if it was moving at hyper speed. Their court house wedding followed by her pregnancy felt like a whirlwind. She rested her hand on her belly, marveling at the fact that there was a life growing inside of her.

She thought of Terry and how he treated his sons. Stacey vowed to never speak or treat her own children that way. She couldn't fathom telling them that they were nothing. Charlie shifted a little in his sleep. Picturing his father with Adele was gross. What kind of man marries a woman like that just to try to get his son to do his bidding? She couldn't wrap her head around it.

Stacey was still worried that things would only get worse from here. She was hoping confronting Terry like this would have shown him how serious his sons were. Instead, it simply backed him into a corner. He lashed out at Eric and was trying to force Charlie to give up his dream. She was sure a shrink would have a field day with Charlie's family.

Eric had gone to his room without them saying a word. Stacey had been so caught up in her thoughts that she had failed to even ask him how he was doing. The brothers hadn't turned on each other in the confrontation with Terry. That counted for something, right?

She decided she'd go make sure Eric wasn't trashing the hotel room. She grabbed her coat and quietly shut the hotel door behind her. The snow covered everything in a thin blanket. Stacey went over and knocked on the door to Eric's room.

There was no answer. Maybe he fell asleep and she was going to wake him up. Even when she thought it, however, she knew that she was wrong. There was no way Eric could calm down enough to let himself rest. He was too wound up. Stacey knocked again when she heard a shuffling noise behind her.

She turned around and saw Eric walking down the pathway toward his room. He carried a small plastic bag from the gas station around the corner. A cigarette hung out of his mouth. The tip glowed dimly in the darkness.

"What are you doing here?" Eric asked her.

"Just wanted to see how you were doing."

Eric held the bag up and it made a clattering noise. "Doing great."

"What's in the bag? Besides probably ten more packs of cigarettes."

"Booze. Now, if you'll excuse me." He walked past her toward the door.

"The room is non-smoking," she pointed to his cigarette.

"Everywhere is non-smoking now," Eric replied, the cigarette still in his mouth.

"So, you're just going to drink tonight?"

Eric stopped looking for his room key and looked up at her. She couldn't read his facial expression. It was completely blank. For some reason, this unsettled her more than if he were angry or irritated with her.

"Why not? You heard dear old Dad. Doesn't really matter what I do. I could do anything I want now because he doesn't expect anything out of me anyway."

"You're going to let what he said affect you like this?" Stacey argued.

Eric sneered, "Please, don't start with me. What am I supposed to do?"

"Live your life. Don't cater to your father anymore. You won't ever please him. Neither you nor Charlie –"

He made a disgusted noise in the back of his throat, "Don't. Don't even compare what Dad said to me to what he said to Charlie. Dad is going to marry Adele just to get Charlie back. In his own warped way, that's the highest compliment he's ever given either one of us. But there isn't anything like that for me, is there? No."

"Eric, I don't think –"

"No, you don't *know*. You don't know anything about my dad, Stacey. My whole life, I've tried to make him think better of me. I did whatever he wanted. I was basically his fucking errand boy. It was pounded into my head that if I only did whatever he wanted, maybe he'd give the company to me instead of Charlie. Well, that didn't happen. Not even close. And you know what? I'm not even fit to run a fucking company worth billions of dollars. Because I was so concerned with impressing Dad that I didn't ever improve myself anywhere else. I didn't learn anything of importance. I did nothing."

Stacey took a step back, unsure of what to say. She didn't expect an outburst like this. For some reason, she thought she was going to be able to speak to him rationally like when she spoke to Charlie.

But the rage in Eric kept spewing forth out of his mouth. "So, while Charlie got everything he ever wanted, I let myself do nothing. That's my own fault. Not Charlie's or my dad's. At any time, I could have told Dad that I wasn't going to do this shit anymore. But I tricked myself. I thought if I got his approval –" His voice caught for a moment and an irritated look crossed his face. "Fuck it. Don't know why I'm telling you this anyway. Besides, I'm smoking. You shouldn't stand near me. Bad for the baby."

He pulled away from her and went over to stand by the edge of the sidewalk, looking at the closed pool. Stacey could only see his back. Eric was hunched over as if he were preparing to run from an attack. His shoulders were tense. Stacey realized he wasn't wearing a coat. He had to have been cold on top of everything else.

The smoke from his cigarette swirled above his head. She watched as he crushed the butt underneath his feet and pulled out another. Stacey went over to him and grabbed his wrist.

"Wait, don't light it yet."

He stared at her and slipped the cigarette in his mouth but didn't light it.

"Eric, please, talk to Charlie about this. You two need a real heart-to heart."

He scoffed, "We need more than a heart-to-heart."

"Then start with it. I know you have a lot of history between the two of you. But if you are both going against Terry and trying to move on from what he has put the two of you through, then you need each other. You're family. You can mend the bridges burned between you two."

"Why? Because you and your sister did?"

"Allison and I had our differences, but we didn't have parents or grandparents like Terry raising us. We just needed to grow up and accept each other for who we are. You and Charlie need to do the same."

"I'm not interested," Eric replied stubbornly.

Stacey stared at him. "Why not?"

"I'm more into self-sabotage," he said darkly.

"I'm afraid I don't follow."

"The night you ended up in the hospital, there was something that I needed to tell you. At the time, I was glad I didn't. But now – fuck it, right? Who cares anymore? I'm leaving town after tonight anyway."

Stacey was still confused as Eric turned around to face her. He tossed the unlit cigarette to the pavement. Her mind was still registering what he said as he grabbed her shoulders firmly and kissed her.

She tasted the cigarette in his mouth. The stubble around his mouth grazed against her skin. Her brain finally caught up to everything that was happening and she pushed against Eric, shoving him off of her.

He stumbled yet didn't try to kiss her again. Stacey felt as if the wind was knocked out of her. She stared at him in shock, unable to speak. Eric's face was blank again. The rage that propelled through him apparently ran out. He bent over and picked up the bag at his feet along with the unlit cigarette.

Then he straightened himself and said, "I had to do that just once."

Before Stacey could reply, he turned and went into his hotel room. She heard the door lock, leaving her alone on the pathway.

Stacey brushed her teeth for the second time in a row. She could still taste Eric's kiss in her mouth – the taste of cigarettes unwilling to leave. She spit the toothpaste into the sink and then took a swig of water.

In the other room, Charlie snored. She gripped the edge of the counter, trying to figure out what to do next. Yet her mind felt as if it was plunged into a fog.

What was it that Charlie told her? *Eric had done this before,* meaning he was accustomed to his brother throwing himself at Charlie's previous girlfriends. At the time, Stacey didn't think much of it. She wasn't like the other girlfriends. She was *married* to his brother. They weren't just a short-term dating situation. She was pregnant with Charlie's baby. For some reason, she thought that meant she wouldn't have to worry about Eric doing something like that.

The night you ended up in the hospital, there was something that I needed to tell you.

Oh no! she thought to herself. He was going to kiss her then, wasn't he? Right after Charlie stormed out, Eric was drunkenly blathering about telling her something. This wasn't something he did on a whim. He had been wanting to do this for some time.

Stacey took the cup of water with her back to the bedroom. She turned on the TV when she came in. It only got two channels. One of them was the weather channel. It was oddly comforting. It reminded her of Tina. She sat at the edge of the bed and stared at the grainy image.

Something else Eric said was nagging in her brain. He said he was into self-sabotage. He must have known kissing her would get back to Charlie. That would ruin any chance of them making amends and becoming close brothers again. Charlie wouldn't want to see Eric anymore, for certain. Eric wouldn't go back to Terry. He'd just drift around on his own. He said he was leaving town, didn't he? He must have assumed that she was going to tell Charlie tonight.

She suddenly felt exhausted. She was supposed to be avoiding stress, but this was not the way to go about it. She finished her water and curled up in bed next to Charlie, who barely stirred when she got in. His back was to her and she gently pressed her hand against his skin.

His skin was warm to the touch and comforting. She was going to have to tell Charlie. Eric played her just right, knowing that there was no way she could keep such a thing from him.

Her eyelids growing heavy, she thought about his last words to her.

I had to do that just once.

Stacey's eyes fluttered open. She was staring at the ceiling of the hotel room. The door shut loudly, jolting her awake. She propped herself up to see Charlie pacing the small room, holding his phone in his hands as he typed.

"What's going on?" she mumbled, still half asleep.

"Eric is gone. I went over there to see how he was doing and the room is empty. I don't know where he is. I'm afraid he went back to Dad's or something. Up to something stupid."

"Charlie..."

Something in her voice caught his attention and he looked up at her, "What?"

"Eric left town."

"How do you know?"

She took a deep breath and then proceeded to tell him the events of last night. When she got to the kiss, Charlie went stiff. His face drained of the little color that was left.

When she finished, Charlie was silent and remained that way for a few moments. He was frozen like a statue. Stacey wondered if the stress had gotten to him and he wasn't going to speak for a while, but just stare ahead at the wall.

"Uh, Charlie?"

"He said what? What did he say?"

She recited what Eric said, but slower, afraid it didn't sink in the first time. When she finished, Charlie shook his head and mumbled *idiot* over and over again.

"What is it? I mean, I know he's an idiot but…"

"Don't you get it? All that talk about self-sabotage and leaving town. He likes you, obviously. And whatever was holding him back from acting on it died when our father pointed out he's a piece of shit. He thinks he's a piece of shit now. So he kissed you and has run off to go do… God knows what."

"I don't think he really feels that way about me," Stacey protested. "He's just confused."

Charlie yanked some clothes out of his bag along with a few toiletries they had bought the night before. "He's confused about nothing. He's just a fucking idiot. You know…for a second – a split second – after everything happened last night, I thought we could fix things." He shook his head.

"You still can. We'll find him and –"

"I don't want to find him. He kissed you, Stacey. You're my wife! I can't trust him around you. If he is so keen on believing the stuff Dad said about him, then let him. I'm not going to track down a brother who's betrayed me yet again and try to convince him to come home."

He stormed out of the room, leaving Stacey in bed. This was what she was afraid of, she thought dully.

She listened to Charlie in the shower and could feel a wave of nausea roll over her. She sucked in air through her mouth and got to her feet, bursting into the bathroom and leaning over the toilet to vomit.

Behind the shower curtain, Charlie stuck his head out, alarmed, "Are you okay?"

"Fine," she mumbled. "Morning sickness."

"No, it's Eric sickness. He's putting you through his own bullshit," Charlie said furiously.

She limply waved her arm for him to stop as another wave washed over her. She didn't want to talk about Eric any longer. Charlie was right about one thing – she was going to stress herself out at this rate. Easier to put it behind her and let Charlie worry about his brother.

Stacey had tried everything she could and all attempts had blown up in her face.

Charlie finished his shower and helped her lie down. She protested, saying she was fine, but he refused to listen.

"We leave in an hour. Just try to get some rest until then," Charlie said sternly to her as he flipped on the TV.

He began to go through the channels and looked confused when it kept cycling through the same two. Stacey, in spite of feeling sickly, laughed. He looked back at her.

"Only two channels," she pointed out. "You gonna be okay with that?"

Charlie smiled at her teasing tone and looked back at the TV. "Guess we're stuck with the weather."

"I don't mind. Tina used to watch it all the time," Stacey replied, shifting so that she could see it better.

"What do you think Tina would say? About all of this? Eric and… my family."

Stacey found the question interesting and thought about it for a few moments before replying, "She would probably find it all ridiculous. And guaranteed she wouldn't want you to give up on Eric."

"Even though he kissed you?"

"She'd say he was lost. She always told me not to brush Allison aside and that we were sisters. She would want you to remember that too. You two are brothers and nothing can change that. You both were loved by your mother and withstood whatever Terry threw at you. I don't think she would want you to give up on him, because he's having a hard time."

Charlie ran his hand over his face, looking tired. "Still doesn't change the fact that he kissed you. And has feelings for you, or whatever he's thinking. I don't care what Dad is doing to make me come back to the company. It doesn't give Eric a free rein to do whatever he wants."

"I know, and I agree. I just don't want you to brush him off completely. He's still your brother."

But Charlie shook his head decisively, "I don't care. I'm done with him."

She wanted to say more but knew at this moment it would be useless. She could see in the set of Charlie's jaw that he was done talking about it. As of right now, he didn't consider Eric to be his brother at all.

Chapter Five

The next two months passed by in a blur. Stacey worked from home, helping William's real estate office as much as she could from the comfort of her living room. Working kept her mind active and gave her a reason to get out of bed in the morning even when she felt incredibly sick from the pregnancy.

Allison was busy helping Jacob after his father's death. With complete control of the tea empire falling to him, her sister was making sure he remembered basic things like eating since he would tend to forget when he was busy. Allison always made sure to come by to see Stacey when she was in town, however, to make sure that everything was going well.

Charlie struggled with getting his company off the ground. The conversation with Terry, as it turned out, didn't matter. By the time he formally left the company, Terry stepped up as temporary president because no one had seen or heard from Eric.

Well, almost no one. A month after he kissed Stacey, Eric sent one postcard to Charlie. It showed a cheesy photo of a cat sleepily lying in a tree. It was post marked from Puerto Rico.

On the back it simply read: *Hanging in there. Hope you're well.*

Charlie threw it out almost immediately. Stacey didn't stop him. She told herself that they would never reconcile. If Eric intended the kiss to ruin things for good, it was a fantastic idea. Charlie undoubtedly meant what he had said in the hotel room – he was done with Eric.

Stacey could hardly believe it was Christmas Eve already. There was a thick blanket of snow that draped the city last week. She worked in the living room, admiring the way the snow looked from this high up.

They decorated their place together and put a giant tree in the living room. A couple weeks ago, Charlie had surprised her with a cat after she said she was a little lonely during the day. The cat, Munchkin, had curled up underneath the tree, sleeping away as Stacey came into the room.

"Ready?" Charlie asked her.

"Yup. Let's go."

Charlie took her hand firmly as they left the penthouse to go see Allison. She was throwing a small Christmas party. Stacey made sure to grab their gifts on the way out and held them tightly.

"You know, it's so weird buying gifts this year. I never know what to get Allison. Some years, I didn't get her anything."

"Why is that?"

"We weren't talking. Or we were fighting about something stupid. The usual. But this year, so much has changed. Allison has everything she ever wanted. So what do I get her?"

"What *did* you get her?" Charlie asked her curiously as they cut across the lobby.

Stacey grinned. "When she was six, there was this limited-edition cupcake maker. It was one of those little oven things where you mix the gross powder and make cakes or something. They had one that made cupcakes and it was too expensive for Mom and Dad to buy for Allison. It had a fancy oven and came with sprinkles and all sorts of extra toppings. Allison was heartbroken that she couldn't get it."

Charlie laughed. "You got her that?"

"I tracked it down online! I mean, hopefully she'll know not to use any of the ingredients or anything. They're all expired. But she's going to totally flip. I know it," Stacey grinned.

He shook his head at her and smiled, "You amaze me."

He leaned in and gave her a kiss before opening the lobby door and getting into the car that pulled up for them. The ride to Allison's place was comfortable, with Stacey bundled up in her coat and listening to Charlie talk about his day.

"And tomorrow, I figured it'd be just the two of us, relaxing," he said as he held her hand. "What do you think?"

Stacey smiled. "Sounds nice. Relaxing. I'm sure Allison will have gone all out tonight so it's better to spend our first Christmas together like that. I just want to relax. Everything has been so crazy lately."

"The entire year has been crazy," Charlie remarked.

Stacey nodded. "A lot has changed. I can hardly believe how quickly everything unfolded."

He nodded and looked lost in thought. Stacey couldn't blame him. The entire year, beginning in the summer, was a whirlwind of events. Strange to think that at the start of the year she was struggling to make enough money at William's diner to pay her bills. And look where everyone was now.

By the time they pulled up to Allison's building, Stacey really needed to pee. Her bladder felt like it was shrinking every day she was pregnant. Charlie took one look at her face as they entered the lobby and laughed.

"Go, go. I'll wait for you here and then we can go up."

"Great, thank you," she said and hurried off toward the restroom.

It was empty for a brief moment before two women burst in. From the stall, Stacey could hear their heels clatter against the tile as they stalked over to the mirror.

"Security was too tight to get to the top floor," one of the women commented, "I thought it'd be busy up there so we could get in but I guess not. Usually Christmas parties are easy to crash."

These two women must have been trying to sneak into Allison's party, Stacey realized. She hadn't even thought about that before – that people would willingly try to get into her sister's parties. Curiously, she stayed still, wondering if they would say anything about why they thought it would be fun to try such a thing.

"So, where are we going next?"

"I think there's a bigger event across town," the first woman replied. "That guy. What was his name?" Stacey heard the woman snap her fingers as if she was trying to jog her memory. "Tony. Tony something."

"The one that was dating Adele?"

"They broke up. She's engaged to some old guy now. I bet one of us could get his interest," the woman said confidently.

"Great. Let's go there, then. If he's hosting a giant party, then I'm game."

Stacey listened as the two women left. Hearing Tony mentioned unexpectedly like that conjured him up in her mind. She hadn't given him much thought after Charlie proposed. This person she was once fond of and seemed like such a kind man; who cornered her in the library one night and frightened her, making her see how controlling he was, was better not to think about.

Even so, Stacey realized that she hadn't thought about him in all of this time for even a brief moment. Was he furious with Adele for leaving him for Charlie's father? There was no way she could have told him it had anything to do with love.

The women in the bathroom sounded as if they knew Adele. They probably ran in the same circle. At the start of this year, Stacey always thought what her sister did with her life was shallow. It never dawned on her that there were probably groups of women who tried to crash parties to find a rich man.

Stacey left the restroom to see Charlie waiting for her. He was checking something on his phone and slipped it in his jacket pocket when she came over.

"Everything okay?" he asked her.

"Yeah. Sorry, there were two women in the ladies' room talking about Tony."

"Mel and Marge. The two M's."

"You know them?" Stacey asked, surprised.

"I saw them coming out. And yes, I know them. They hung out with Adele a lot."

"They tried to get into Allison's party, apparently. Now they're going to try to woo Tony," Stacey explained as they headed over to the elevator.

"Good luck with that."

Something in his tone got Stacey's attention. "What do you mean?"

Charlie avoided her stare. "Heard he wasn't doing very well, that's all." He pressed the button on the elevator to take them to Allison's place.

Stacey blinked and followed him into the elevator. "What do you mean?"

"Well, Adele dumped him for my dad. You saw him that night at the library. I've never seen him like that before. And everything else you told me… how he acted on the island. How keen he was on trying to find someone his parents were interested in…"

"I'm not following."

Charlie shrugged. "Just heard that he parties a lot now. I wouldn't let it concern you. Tony made his bed and has to lie in it now. If he's lost his head over his weird fixation on finding someone to marry, that's his issue."

Stacey leaned against the elevator wall as it took them up. "He did seem fixated on it."

"He's always been like that. I don't know why. He probably thought he had you and then I fucked it up. Then he probably thought he had Adele. He never spoke of her very kindly before. But she was always willing to marry anyone who could tolerate her."

"He wanted his family to approve of whomever he married. He wouldn't go with Adele. There is no way that his parents would approve."

"Adele already met his family a couple of years back. She got along great with them. They loved her. But, mind you, she was a completely different person around them. She met them a few times at social events. He would have married her if she had stuck it out a bit longer."

Stacey thought about this as they walked into Allison's place. Adele changing herself to have people like her didn't come as a surprise. It was more surprising that Tony was partying a lot lately. He never struck her as the type.

There was a dark side to him that she saw that night in the library, and flashes of it when she ran away to his island. She was safe, Stacey thought to herself, now that she was away from Tony. Let him have his parties and his billions of dollars. She would have never been happy with him.

Allison saw them immediately when they entered the party and swooped over to them. She wore a pinched expression on her face and practically cornered the two of them.

"Are you okay?" Stacey asked her curiously.

"I didn't invite him," she said.

For a wild second, Stacey thought her sister meant Tony. It would be just her luck, wouldn't it, that one of her ex-boyfriends appeared at this party. But Charlie seemed to understand exactly what Allison was saying because he pushed past her into the penthouse.

"What is it?" Stacey asked her.

But Allison was chasing after Charlie in her stiletto heels. Confused, Stacey slipped out of her jacket and hung it up. She looked into the living room and was greeted by William, Amanda, and Brad, whom she wasn't expecting but was thrilled to see. Jacob was in the middle of the room, talking to someone she didn't know.

Stacey hadn't seen Jacob in a while. He looked thinner than usual and there were circles around his eyes. Allison mentioned that he was taking his father's death harder than even he had expected. She could hear him speaking now. His voice sounded quieter than usual. She waved at him as she walked by and he acknowledged her with a nod.

Amanda came over and hugged her gently. "Sorry, I'm hyper paranoid about hurting the baby but I had to hug you. I only ever talk to you on the phone now or through e-mail. I never get to see you!"

"Believe me, it's pretty dull to be working from home."

"Better to be resting and working from home than overdoing it at the office," William said seriously.

"Even so, I want to talk a little business with you."

"Come on, Stacey, it's a party," Brad protested.

Stacey smiled. "You're right, you're right. Christmas Eve and all." She sighed, "Could you excuse me a moment. I'll be back." She rushed off in search of the bathroom. The baby was really dancing on her bladder this evening.

She crossed the living room and went down the nearest hallway which had a guest room and a bathroom. She grabbed the handle, but it was locked. She bobbed on the balls of her feet, considering if she should go to the other bathroom near Allison's room. This place was spread out and there was no need to wait here for the door to open.

As she turned around to leave, the door opened. Her heart felt as if it stopped for a moment.

Out came Eric.

Chapter Six

Allison's apology of 'I didn't invite him' floated back to Stacey and it all finally clicked. She didn't mean Tony, she meant Eric. He was standing in front of her with a bored expression on his face. He wore a rumpled white button-up shirt that was a size too large for him. The sleeves hung over his wrists as if he were a child playing dress up with his father's clothes.

"Eric!" Stacey said, surprised.

"That's my name," Eric deadpanned, moving past her.

He didn't say anything else. She watched him saunter off down the hallway back into the fray of the party. Stacey headed into the bathroom and closed the door behind her. She couldn't believe that he was here.

All hopes of the party being enjoyable and Charlie having a relaxing time was out the window. She was expecting Charlie to punch Eric in the face as soon as he saw him. Her only hope was that he wouldn't do it at the party, but would wait until they were alone.

She finished quickly, washed her hands and headed back to join the party. Allison was by her side within a few seconds.

"Where did you go?" asked Allison.

She shook her head when Stacey tried to reply.

"I don't care, please, just keep Charlie occupied and make sure he doesn't murder his brother in front of everyone."

Stacey nodded and walked into the dining room. There were a few more people that she didn't know there. Charlie was on the balcony, staring out at the city. Eric was in the corner of the dining room. Stacey did a double take.

There was a woman with her arms draped around Eric. She was a platinum blonde, shorter than he was, wearing a baggy t-shirt and cut off denim shorts, noticeably dressed down from everyone else at the party. How was she not freezing to death? On top of that, she was wearing red platform heels that must have been six inches high. For a moment, Stacey wondered if Eric brought a prostitute or a stripper to the party just to cause trouble.

Eric's gaze flicked around the room before stopping at Stacey. He motioned for her to come over. When she took a step away instead to go toward Charlie, Eric tugged his date toward her.

"Stacey," he said. "This is my date, Kailyn."

Stacey thought she misheard, "Kailyn?"

"Yes, that's right," the woman, Kailyn, trilled in a loud voice. "Pleasure to meet you!"

They shook hands. Kailyn was wearing a strong perfume that made Stacey's eyes water. She took a small step back hoping to avoid the invisible perfume cloud that seemed to engulf the woman.

Up close, Eric's lady friend looked a bit older than she did from afar. There were deep lines around her eyes and her lips looked a size too large to be natural. She looked as if she had stepped out of a comic book. It hardly felt as if Stacey was looking at a real person.

Eric watched her with a detached expression on his face. She had no idea what he was thinking. Why did he turn up out of nowhere like this?

"It's lovely to meet you," Stacey lied, smiling. "I just have to speak with my husband for a moment. I'll be back later."

Kailyn nodded and said something so quickly that Stacey couldn't even make it out. She was thankful for the fresh air when she got outside. Charlie stared blankly at the city. Stacey approached and stood next to him.

"Okay," she said slowly, "what the hell is that about?"

"Which part? Eric coming back and crashing Allison's party or the fact he brought someone who belongs on a reality show?"

"Both, I guess."

He shook his head. "No idea. I avoided him as soon as I saw him. Whatever reason he has for coming back isn't anything I want to be a part of."

"He's going to try to talk to you eventually," Stacey pointed out.

"Let him. I'm not causing a scene at your sister's party."

"Good. Because she asked me to make sure of that."

"Nah, not here."

Stacey rubbed his back, unsure of what to say. She had been looking forward to a relaxing evening. Eric appearing with a date named Kailyn wasn't exactly her idea of a fantastic Christmas Eve. She felt irritation blooming in her chest and tried to ignore it.

"Maybe he came here to apologize or make things right." Even as the words left her mouth, however, she knew they weren't true. That wasn't Eric's style.

Charlie scoffed in reply and didn't say anything else. She could practically see the dark cloud over her husband's head.

"Well, just don't pay any attention to him. I ran into him in the hallway and he barely even spoke to me. Even when he introduced Kailyn –"

"Wait, wait. Kailyn?"

"Yeah, that's her name, apparently."

Charlie sighed, "Really? Kailyn? Where the hell did he find her?"

"I don't know. She seems uh… nice," she said almost apologetically.

Charlie laughed at this and threw his arm around her, bringing her in close. She could smell the cologne on him – a welcome scent after Kailyn's cloying perfume. She closed her eyes and for a few seconds, everything washed away. There was just her, Charlie and their child.

"You always want to see the good in people. I wish I could be similar."

"There has to be a time when you and Eric got along," she said, her words muffled by his jacket which he still hadn't removed.

He looked down at her. "Maybe before our mom died. I remember us wearing socks that were too big. I think they were our dad's. Anyway, we use to slide around on the floor in his socks. We'd pretend we were in martial arts films."

Stacey tried to picture it but it proved to be impossible. She couldn't imagine the two brothers sliding around the floor like that, laughing and having fun. Instead, the memory of them being drunk together at the last party floated in her head. She could see them with their heads bent together, laughing hysterically as they stuck that sticker on Jacob.

"You have a lighter?"

Charlie released his arm from Stacey as she stood back and looked behind them. Eric stood there. She could see dark circles under his eyes that mirrored Jacob's. Only he wasn't dealing with his father dying like Jacob was – so why was he so tired?

"Why would I have a lighter?" Charlie said roughly.

Eric shrugged and turned behind him. "Babe, I need a lighter."

Kailyn teetered up to him in her heels and pulled out a silver lighter. She bent over and lit the tip of Eric's cigarette, smiling at him the entire time. He took a drag from his cigarette and waved the smoke away from his face.

"Thanks. This is my brother, Charlie. He's married to Stacey."

Kailyn turned to look at Charlie who had a funny expression on his face. It was half irritation and half trying not to laugh. The end result made his mouth twist in a strange manner.

"You're Eric's brother? I've heard so much about you!" she exclaimed loudly. "All nice things, naturally. Anyway, he said you're starting your own business! How exciting!"

This woman, Kailyn, was drunk, Stacey realized. She was so caught up in Eric appearing here that she didn't notice it at first. Yet in front of her, Kailyn swayed uncertainly on her feet and her eyes looked glassy.

"How long have you been seeing Eric?" Charlie asked kindly.

"Uhhhh…," she dragged it out as she thought, sucking on her bottom lip. "Like a week?"

"Wow, a whole week," Charlie remarked although Kailyn was too drunk to notice the dig, "Amazing. How did you two meet?"

"I was a waitress at this diner down south that Eric stopped by almost every day just to see me. And then he said he was going back home and wanted to know if I wanted to come with him and how could I resist that?" She slurred a little at the final word but otherwise was masking her voice well enough.

"Romantic," Charlie quipped, and Stacey nudged him with her elbow in a silent voice of 'be nice'.

Kailyn beamed at the two of them but before she could say anything else, Eric spoke up, "Honey, can you get me another drink?"

She nodded and left to go back into the penthouse. They watched her go and when she was out of ear shot, it was Charlie who spoke first.

"Honestly, what the hell are you doing?"

"What, you don't like her?" Eric asked and then waved his hand around his face. "Fuck, sorry, Stacey. The baby."

"You could put the cigarette out, you know," Charlie snapped.

"I could but I really want this," he replied stubbornly.

"It's okay. I'll go," Stacey said even though she didn't like the idea of leaving the brothers alone.

She made her way back into the penthouse. Christmas music was playing now, although her festive mood seemed to have vanished. Kailyn had gotten distracted on the way to another drink and was talking to Brad who was looking as if he were talking to a side show exhibit.

What was the deal with Eric just bringing someone like Kailyn to this event? Was that what he was doing all these months – just shacking up with various women and taking them around with him? If so, Kailyn was probably the feather in his cap. There was no way she'd fit in here. Eric probably didn't even care for her too much.

Stacey suddenly felt bad for the woman. Out of her element, already drunk – there were probably more issues with Kailyn than she was letting on. Maybe it was her motherly protective urges kicking in, but she made her way over to Kailyn.

"Hey, what's up?" she asked nicely.

Brad raised his eyebrows. "Uh, not much. Kailyn… Kailyn?" When she nodded to confirm her name, he went on, "Kailyn was just telling me about how she's dating your brother-in-law."

"That's right. Actually, Kailyn, I'd love to hear more about how that has been. Why don't we go over here?" She linked arms with the woman.

She nodded and Stacey was able to steer her away from Brad, who mouthed a 'thank you' to her. She led Kailyn into another room that had a pool table and a bar. A TV was on, playing some sports program that three men were watching. They didn't pay the two of them any attention. She allowed Kailyn to seat herself on a couch in the back of the room before sitting down next to her.

"So, Eric, huh? Must be fun," Stacey remarked, hoping she didn't sound phony.

If she did, Kailyn didn't notice and replied, "So much fun. He said he'd take care of everything money-wise. Which is good because I'm low on funds right now. It's been a pretty crazy week."

"What have you guys been up to?"

"Drinking, mostly. Partying. Eric knows where all the great parties are. You know, he didn't mention a brother until last night though. And I was like 'oh why is that?' and he said his brother was a jerk but he seemed quite nice out there! No offense. You're married to his brother, right?"

"Ah, yeah but it's fine. No offense taken. He didn't say why he decided to come back here?"

Kailyn shook her head and her snowman earrings bobbed against her thin neck. "Nope. He doesn't like to talk too much about the past."

"What about you? I mean, it's Christmas Eve. No family to stay with?"

Kailyn leaned over Stacey and grabbed a drink that was left on the table. Stacey was about to suggest getting a fresh one, but Kailyn downed the remaining whiskey in one gulp before settling back down on the couch.

"Didn't want it to go to waste," she explained before saying, "No. My parents are dead. I was an only child. Been working at that diner for years and years. Figured well, why the fuck not? Eric has money, too. Did you know that?"

"Yes."

"That's right, sorry," Kailyn replied. "Anyway, when a rich man wants to take me around the town, I'm not going to say no!"

Stacey nodded in agreement but something nagged at the back of her mind. She felt as if the hairs on the back of her neck were standing up. Dead end job. Parents dead. The only difference was Kailyn was an only child. Stacey was staring at herself in an alternate universe.

"Will you excuse me for a moment?" she said quickly, standing up.

"Yeah, tell Eric I'm in here, will you? Do you think the woman who owns this place would care if we snuck off somewhere?" The implication of what 'sneaking off' meant was clear.

"Probably, yes," Stacey said, and left the room, heading back to find Charlie and Eric.

Chapter Seven

The brothers weren't on the balcony. Stacey turned around and discovered Allison standing next to her. She jumped in surprise.

"How do you do that? You're just magically appearing everywhere tonight," Stacey remarked.

"What's the deal with that woman Eric brought? Is he dating her? Has he lost his mind?"

"Yes and yes."

Allison clicked her tongue against the roof of her mouth. "She looks like she's on something. Where is she?"

"Wanting Eric to fuck her in one of your rooms. Don't look at me like that! I told her you would mind."

"Oh, that'll show her," Allison scoffed and marched off to probably go drag Kailyn into her line of sight.

Stacey watched her go and sighed. She went into the kitchen to see if Charlie and Eric were in there. Amanda was in the corner talking to Brad. William got sucked into a conversation with Jacob and looked like he was falling asleep on the spot.

She went over to Amanda and Brad. "Have you guys seen Charlie?"

"Yeah, they went to the other side of the penthouse. This place is massive. I feel like I'd get lost and be found, like, a week later starving to death," Brad remarked.

"Thanks," she said quickly and hurried out of the kitchen.

Always this hallway, Stacey thought to herself as she walked down past the bathroom where she had started bleeding and past the library where Tony had grabbed her. She made a mental note to tell her sister that this side of the place was cursed or something.

She stopped in front of one of the guest rooms. She could hear voices and opened the door, hoping it wasn't the two people she dreaded them to be.

It wasn't. Inside, Charlie had Eric pinned against the wall and was raising his fist as if to punch him. Stacey cried out and ran over, grabbing his arm. Charlie looked back in surprise. Eric took advantage of this and pushed Charlie hard. He toppled backward onto the bed.

Stacey reached out and grabbed Eric, trying to tug him away from his brother. But he shrugged her off and tackled Charlie.

Stacey stood and watched the two grown men wrestle like children on the bed. There was a solid thud of Charlie's fist connecting with Eric's shoulder, who grunted in return and kicked Charlie off the bed. He hit the floor and Eric lunged after him.

Sibling rivalries were the worst, Stacey declared to herself. They turned grown adults into children, no matter the age. There was no way she was going to get in the middle of the fray. The last thing she needed was to trip and fall in her condition. She felt weary of both Charlie and Eric in that moment.

Maybe they just needed to wrestle like absolute idiots together. Stacey took a step back with her back against the door and crossed her arms. She was mentally forming a lecture in her head when Charlie finally stood up.

"Enough!" he strained through a ragged breath. "Get off me!" He pushed Eric away when he tried to swing another punch.

"Are you two finished?" Stacey said in a clipped tone. "Honestly, you guys aren't twelve anymore."

"He kissed you!" Charlie exclaimed. "I've been wanting to punch him ever since!"

He jerked his arms as if to gesture to Eric. But Eric's head was bent, looking down at something on his shirt. Charlie's elbow accidently slammed into Eric's nose and sent him jolting back.

"Fuck!" he exclaimed in surprise.

Blood gushed out of his nose all over the white button-up shirt. It bloomed across his chest like roses.

Charlie began to apologize but Eric jerked away from him in irritation.

It was then that someone tried to get into the bedroom. Stacey was pushed forward as Allison wedged her way into the room.

"What the fuck is going on in here?! It sounds like people are either fucking or murdering each other!" she snapped in irritation, looking around the room. When her eyes landed on Eric bleeding, she huffed.

"Allison, let me explain –" Charlie began, but his sister-in-law raised her hand up to fend him off.

"No, I don't want to hear it. If you weren't married to my sister, I'd kick you out. No offense, Charlie, but you're always a handful at my parties."

He opened his mouth as if to protest but thought better of it and closed it instead.

"And you, Eric – you weren't even invited. So take yourself, your bleeding nose and your weird girlfriend and please leave," Allison said firmly.

Eric covered his nose but the blood kept dripping through his fingers. Allison turned around and left, shutting the door behind her. Stacey went over to the two of them and led Eric into the ensuite bathroom.

Behind her, Charlie spoke. "I didn't mean to connect like that. It was an accident."

"Does it matter?" Stacey asked tiredly. "You two were fighting like little kids anyway. Come here, Eric."

She tore off a wad of toilet paper and had him try to stop the bleeding. His shirt looked as if he had been in a bar fight. She made a clucking noise as Eric held the toilet paper against his nose.

"Go lie down on the bed," she ordered him.

Without any protest, he moved past Charlie and flopped down on the bed they were just fighting on, holding the tissue against his nose. Then she turned to Charlie.

"What is wrong with you two? This is how you settle differences? Fist fighting? This isn't some playground spat. I left you alone before and you two were talking. What the hell happened?"

From the bed, muffled due to his nose, Eric spoke up, "He's a dick."

"No, that isn't a reason. You two need to actually hold a conversation and work things out. How long are you going to do this for?"

"He kissed you, Stacey. Why am I supposed to forgive him for that?" Charlie protested. "We tried to speak and he's just – he's impossible to talk to! He isn't going to change."

"Me?" Eric protested from the bed. "Why do I have to change? You need to change… asshole."

"You're the one who couldn't handle Dad being mean to you so you've spent months running away, probably drinking and fucking your way around the country!" Charlie said.

"Enough! This is exactly what I mean!" Stacey exclaimed. "This isn't a conversation. It's just fighting. Charlie, I know. I know what he did, okay. But Eric knew what he was doing too. He knew kissing me was just a way to ruin things," she lowered her voice. "He knew he could run away then. It gave him a way out."

Charlie exhaled slowly as if fending off the urge to go over and punch Eric again, who was lying silently on the bed, waiting for his nose to stop bleeding.

"You two can't keep doing this," she said.

"Why not? Looks to be working just fine," Eric replied, his voice sounding clogged.

Stacey turned to look at him. "You aren't helping things and you know it. Whatever you went through since Terry said those things to you – you can't just sit on them forever. Is this what you want? To be absolved from doing anything because your father said you were nothing? Makes life easier, doesn't it? You can go anywhere you want and not be expected to do anything because of your father. And when you're bored, you come back here and cause trouble. That's what you want life to be?"

Eric didn't reply. He was very still on the bed. Stacey turned back to Charlie.

"You're going to be a father soon. Is that what you want your child seeing? At this rate, you and Eric won't have any relationship at all, which means our child won't have an uncle. Are you okay with that?"

Charlie didn't reply right away. He just stared at her, wide-eyed, before he mumbled, "I hadn't considered that."

"No, of course not." She shook her head and walked toward the door. "I'm going to spend some time with Allison. Eric, you should leave once your nose is done bleeding or she'll flip."

With that, she closed the door behind her.

Chapter Eight

When Charlie and Stacey got home that night, she could feel that he wanted to talk about what happened. But Stacey didn't feel like it. She was tired. Her feet were sore. She had spent most of the party on her feet, clinging to Allison as if she could ward off the bad vibes of Charlie and Eric.

She had seen Eric take Kailyn by the hand and leave twenty minutes later. Kailyn had protested, trying to explain that she wanted another drink. By this time, she was so drunk that Stacey couldn't understand how she was even standing.

Charlie, as if sensing her mood, had kept a safe distance from her for the rest of the party. He probably thought she was angry. The truth was that Stacey wasn't angry – just mostly tired.

Yet she couldn't help but wonder why she was putting so much energy into Charlie's familial problems. Perhaps she saw something of how she and Allison used to be in them. She thought if Allison could become someone she eventually grew to have such a great relationship with, surely Charlie could get that way with Eric.

But, she thought, as she took her shoes off in the entranceway of their home, it was time to focus on her pregnancy and getting ready for the baby's arrival. She was putting too much energy into getting the two brothers to be friendly to each other.

"Can I get you anything?" Charlie asked her.

"Just a water, actually. Thanks," she replied as she plopped down onto the couch.

A minute later, Charlie returned with a bottle of water. She took it, mumbling a 'thanks' and opened it. He sat down next to her. For a split second, he looked like a child waiting for a lecture. If Stacey didn't feel so tired, she would have found it funny.

Munchkin was under the tree, sleeping soundly. Stacey wished she could be a cat. Imagine just sleeping anywhere like that.

"Can we talk about Eric?"

She sighed, "I'm tired, Charlie. Physically tired and also just in general about your brother."

"He has that effect on people," he replied and when he saw the warning look on her face, he cleared his throat. "I mean, just... like, he has a lot of effects on people."

"Nice save." She rolled her eyes.

"Maybe I haven't been... trying as hard as I could be. With Eric. Although, I don't know if I should be the one making all the effort, because he did kiss you. I don't think I've mentioned that enough."

"You might have brought it up like, once or twice," Stacey joked.

Charlie ran his fingers through his hair. "I didn't mean to make him bleed. I was holding back that entire fight. I could have really decked him if I wanted to."

"So kind of you," she replied dryly.

"Come on, I don't get a little credit for that?"

"For not pummeling your brother senseless at my sister's Christmas Eve party?"

"Well, when you word it like that…" He cleared his throat. "There's history with my brother. Nothing good."

"I already know this, Charlie," she said with a sigh. "Honestly, I can't stand having this conversation yet again. I meant what I said earlier. Think of it this way – if you two don't work out your grievances, then your father won here too. Do you want that?"

She stood up, ready for bed. Charlie didn't say anything. Before she left she paused, looked back at him, and sighed.

"I'm not angry. You know that, right? But I can't just keep going around in circles about Eric. I know what he did. I know it was a shitty thing to do. But I also know that he reminds you of your mother. You said that's why Terry has an issue with him, but what about you?"

A funny look crossed Charlie's face. Stacey shrugged, too weary to say anything. Then she turned around and headed to the bedroom to sleep.

In her dream that night, she was at Terry's manor. It was storming outside and the power had been knocked out. Stacey was walking down the stairs to get to the living room. For some reason, she knew Charlie was down there with her child. She could hear them whispering. Her steps quickened.

Yet when she got to the living room, it was empty. Stacey looked around for them but they weren't there. A sudden noise made her turn around. Eric was standing in the doorway. His shirt was covered in blood and he was smoking a cigarette.

"Looking for your kid?" he said to her and when she nodded, he said, "No idea. Can't see the kid, remember?"

Stacey looked to the right to see that long hallway again. There was a door at the end. She headed toward it, knowing that Charlie was there. Someone reached out and grabbed her wrist, yanking her back.

"What are you doing?" It was Eric.

"I have to go," Stacey said, although her words came out slowly and slurred.

"They don't want to see you. They don't want you as a part of their lives any longer. You're stuck here with me."

Alarmed, she tried to pull away from Eric's hand. But his grip was iron-tight, and he didn't budge. With his free hand, he held out a cigarette.

"Want one?"

Stacey felt a wail swell in her throat – a panicked cry at never seeing Charlie and her child again –

"I'm here, I'm here. It's just a dream!" Charlie's arms were around her and she woke up with her face pressed into his neck.

For a second, she was still in the dream with Eric pulling on her wrist. She could smell the cigarette smoke wafting off of him and tried to push herself away.

"Stacey, it's me! You're awake!" he exclaimed.

His voice cut through the dream fog that was still wafting within her brain. She took a deep breath and stopped trying to break free. Charlie moved so that he could see her face. It was dark in the room but she could make out the outline of his jaw and his eyes on hers.

"Just a dream," he repeated and kissed her gently.

"S-sorry. Sorry. I woke you up again. I'm sorry," she blathered.

"No, it's fine. Do you need anything? Some water?"

Now that he mentioned it, she was feeling parched. It was as if she had crossed the desert or something. She nodded and he slid out of bed, going into the bathroom and coming back with a glass of water.

She drank it quickly and could feel her heart beat slowing down.

"Dreams have been more vivid since I got pregnant."

"I wish you could have dreams of you just watching TV or reading… something mellow," Charlie said.

"Me too. There's always something just out of reach or I'm being kept away from something." Even now, the dream was fading and no matter how hard she tried, it was harder to cling to the images that had terrorized her before.

"Can I help you relax?" Charlie asked her, brushing a lock of her hair off her face.

"I might watch some TV. I don't think I'll be able to sleep."

"I have a different idea."

Something in his tone caught her attention. She turned to look at him. He leaned forward and kissed her gently on the lips.

She shook her head. "Charlie, I don't –"

"I don't mean that," he whispered in her ear.

Stacey didn't follow until his hand slid under her pajama bottoms and trailed across the front of her underwear. The sudden touch sent a shock through her. It had been a while since they had fooled around. Charlie, after working long hours, would come home exhausted and fall promptly asleep. Some nights, Stacey just wasn't feeling up to it. To feel his touch now sparked something inside of her.

Charlie gently pressed her down against the bed and moved her underwear aside. His fingers were warm and probed along her skin. She closed her eyes, letting the feeling of him wash over her.

One of his fingers slid gently inside of her. He moved it around, letting her get used to the sensation. She could hear Charlie breathing in her ear as he pumped his finger inside of her.

Then his finger was gone. Alarmed, she opened her eyes, wanting to protest. But Charlie pressed his lips to hers before he began to slide down her body. She felt him tug off her pajama bottoms.

His finger trailed down the front of her pussy again and then he slowly lowered her panties. In the darkness, she could just make out his head down by her thighs. She felt butterfly kisses along her thighs which caused goosebumps to pebble her skin.

Then Charlie flicked his tongue along her wetness, causing her to gasp in surprise. The sensation was so sudden that she raised her hips slightly. Charlie took that as a sign she wanted more.

Gripping her thighs, Charlie began to flick his tongue along her clit. Stacey let out a small moan as his tongue flicked and rolled over her clit. His fingers dug into her thighs as he moved his tongue around her wet pussy.

Then, one of his fingers entered her. He alternated between pumping his finger inside of her and rolling his tongue across her clit. Sliding a second finger inside of her, Stacey's hips bucked as she felt her orgasm mounting.

Charlie was buried in between her thighs with his tongue moving swiftly along her pussy. Two fingers were moving in and out of her quickly, hitting just the right spot, her G-spot. Her entire body tingled with pleasure.

He wrapped his lips around her clit and jammed his fingers deep inside of her. As he continued to massage her pleasure spot, Stacey felt an urge to pee. She tensed up momentarily, causing Charlie to look up and say, "Let it go. It's okay. Give in to this."

Trusting Charlie's words, she relaxed and gave in to the sensation. Charlie continued the rhythmic massage with his two fingers and lapping at her clit with his tongue.

That was enough to send her over the edge. Stacey moaned loudly as her love juices flowed freely, practically squirting into Charlie's mouth. Her entire body shuddered as she felt her orgasm spasm through her whole being. Charlie kept his face down there, moving his fingers still deep inside her.

The sensation was so intense as the waves of pleasure rolled through her that Stacey went limp immediately afterward. She had never experienced a deep G-spot orgasm before. He moved away from her and slid up to kiss her. She could taste herself on him and she kissed him passionately. Already her eyes were trying to close. She could feel sleep coming for her.

Against her skin, she could feel Charlie smile and she knew all was right in the world. He kissed the top of her head and sleep came for her swiftly.

Christmas morning was a quiet affair. Charlie told Stacey she could invite anyone she wanted, yet she opted for spending it with him and their cat. He gave her a beautiful necklace. In return, Stacey gave him a sweater she knitted during the time she had been resting.

"I didn't even know you took up knitting," he said as he held up the sweater.

"It was a secret. You could buy anything you want so I decided to make you something one-of-a-kind."

He smiled and said, "I love it," as he slipped it on.

It was a little large but Charlie said he didn't care. He brought her in for a big kiss before asking, "What did Allison think of the gift?"

"She said she was going to open it today. I think she was too annoyed with how the party unfolded to open any gifts. I'm sure she'll call me when she does."

"Well, what do you want for dinner tonight? I'll cook everything."

Stacey cringed. "Last time you cooked, dinner was a disaster."

It was true. Charlie had made dinner a month ago. It was supposed to be a surprise for her, but he practically burnt the kitchen down.

"That was just an unfortunate pasta related incident," Charlie said, as if reading her mind.

Stacey laughed. "Oh, is that what we're calling it now?"

He grinned when the elevator doors dinged, alerting them to someone coming in. Alarmed, Charlie got up and went over to see who it was. Stacey couldn't imagine who would be coming to their home on Christmas Day.

She hurried after Charlie and watched in surprise as, of all people, his father, Terry, stepped in, followed by Adele.

"Merry fucking Christmas," she heard Charlie mumble under his breath.

Chapter Nine

Terry and Adele were followed by Eric and Kailyn. The sight of all of them in their home was a shock. Stacey could tell by the look on Charlie's face that he was not expecting this either.

Terry looked as if he had aged ten years since the last time she saw him. He was hunched over and clutching his cane. Adele was helping him by resting one arm on his shoulder as if to steer him. Was Stacey imagining things or did she have dark circles under her eyes?

Behind them, Eric looked just as exhausted. Kailyn was exclaiming loudly about how nice the foyer looked. Her high heels lit up when they hit the floor, Stacey noticed, and she was pretty sure they were something only strippers wore.

Charlie went up to them and said, "This is a surprise. What do I owe this… pleasure?" He paused on the last word as he looked over at his brother.

"Dad here surprised me at the hotel I was staying at," Eric replied. "Said he wanted to spend Christmas with us. He came by this morning."

He looked over at Terry but it was Adele who said, "He wanted it to be a surprise. So we didn't call you."

"What if we'd had plans?" Charlie crossed his arms.

At this Terry snorted, "I knew you'd be holed up in here with your wife."

He pushed past Charlie to go farther into the penthouse. Charlie's face turned to stone as he turned back to look at Eric. The two of them were whispering now but Stacey couldn't hear anything they were saying.

Terry and Adele stopped in front of her. Terry mumbled a greeting before heading over to the kitchen. Stacey watched him go at a snail's pace. Then she turned back to Adele who was wrinkling her nose.

"Do you have a cat in here?"

"Yes. Why?"

"I'm allergic," Adele replied, offended at the mere idea that there was a cat in the same space as her.

"That's a real shame," Stacey said. "Guess you'll have to spend Christmas elsewhere."

Irritation flickered across Adele's eyes and she pressed her lips into a thin line. "No, I'm fine."

"Great," Stacey drawled as she took off to follow Terry, who sounded as if he was rummaging around in the kitchen.

Kailyn came over to her and crushed her in a hug as if they were best friends. Her eyeliner was smudged, and she smelled of whisky and that same perfume she had worn the night before. The scent made Stacey's eyes water.

"Merry Christmas!" she said in Stacey's ear before heading off into the kitchen.

Stacey went over to Charlie and Eric. Their heads were bowed together as if they were almost praying. They didn't seem to be fighting at all. It was a strange sight. Stacey lowered her voice to ask what the hell was going on.

Eric replied, "It was exactly as I said. Dad stopped by out of the blue. Adele was with him and said he wanted to spend Christmas with us. I told him that was a bad idea, but he said he was going over anyway and I could either come along or not. So, I came because I thought it'd be better than just having Dad come after you."

"Why didn't you call me?"

"I did!" Eric protested. "Your phone went straight to voicemail."

"Shit, I forgot to charge it last night." Charlie rubbed his face with his hands before turning to Stacey. "What do you want to do?"

"We can't kick them out. It's Christmas."

"It's also my dad."

"Yeah but," Stacey looked over her shoulder and lowered her voice. "There has to be a reason he came here. Think about it. You haven't heard from him in months and he shows up for Christmas?"

Eric begrudgingly said, "She has a point."

"Why did you have to bring Kailyn?" Charlie asked Eric.

"Hey listen, don't get mad at me for that. She was with me when Dad came over. What am I supposed to say?"

"You need to break up with her," Stacey remarked.

He looked at her, surprised. "Why?"

"Come on. She's a mess, first off. And I know you only brought her here to piss off Charlie." Stacey crossed her arms.

Eric looked abashed. "I will. After this trip, okay? I'm not going to dump her now. Not when Dad is here. He's going to loathe her."

"What a beautiful relationship you have," Charlie replied.

Eric shrugged and moved past the two of them before turning around and saying, "Let's go enjoy Christmas with our father."

Stacey watched him go into the kitchen and looked over at Charlie. His lips were tightly pressed and he looked as if he wanted to go right to bed. Munchkin appeared at the end of the hallway and sauntered down toward them.

"Adele said she's allergic to cats," Stacey remembered out loud to Charlie as she scooped up Munchkin.

"Great, maybe she'll have to leave sooner," Charlie replied as he turned to look at her. "Do you really think Dad has another reason for being here?"

"Yes. It's not like him, correct? There has to be a reason he showed up. Just don't lose your cool and try to stay on Eric's side. If he sees that you two are getting along, it might throw a wrench in his plans."

He nodded and took a deep breath, "Alright. Let's go."

He reached over and grabbed Stacey's hand. Together, they went into the kitchen. Kailyn cornered Eric by the fridge and threw her arms around his neck. She was cooing in his ear. Eric's arm was around her waist and he was mumbling in her ear. It felt as if Stacey walked into the beginning of a pornographic film.

Terry stared at them in distaste but didn't say anything, which was shocking enough. Stacey cleared her throat.

Eric turned his head. "Well, I could go for a Bloody Mary."

A scowl crossed Terry's face. "Drinking already?" he remarked.

"Come on, Dad, it's like nine in the morning. An hour later than I usually start," Eric replied as he pulled out everything to make the drinks.

Stacey was taken back to that morning in the manor when Charlie left to go into town with Terry. It was one of the first times that she had been around Eric. A sense of déjà vu washed over her. It was the sight of Charlie looking at his father warily and Eric making a drink just to get under Terry's skin that propelled her forward.

"What would you like to drink?" she directed this to Terry who eyed her warily.

"Coffee."

"Great, I'll make you some." She moved toward the coffee machine, aware that Terry was watching her.

"Charlie, you want a Bloody Mary?" Eric asked him over his shoulder.

Stacey couldn't help but flick her gaze over to her husband. This was it, she thought to herself. Was Charlie going to show a united front with Eric or not? She found herself holding her breath as she turned away to pull down the coffee from the cupboard above her head.

"Yes," Charlie replied, "I'll take one."

She looked over at Eric, who donned what could only be described as a 'shit-eating grin' on his face. "Wonderful."

She heard Terry make a disgusted sound in his throat, "Really, boy?"

Charlie ignored him and looked at Stacey, "You got the coffee?"

"Yup! You know, I think we have some pastries over there. We can all snack on those and catch up."

Kailyn clasped her hands together and chimed, "Eric, make me a drink too, will you?"

"Of course. Drinks for everyone. Except for Stacey, for obvious reasons."

Stacey turned back to the coffee machine and tried to hide the smile that was forming on her face.

They settled in around the dining room table. The pastries were placed in the center along with a carafe of coffee. Adele was perched at the end of her chair as if she was getting ready to flee at any sign of their cat. Kailyn was drinking her Bloody Mary as if she was suffering from dehydration. Terry was seated and looking shrunken. There was an odd expression on his face that Stacey had never seen before. He looked almost uncertain. Could he ever be uncertain?

Yet it was Charlie and Eric who looked the most at ease. Eric was leaning back in the chair, wobbling on the back legs. It was the sort of thing a child did to irritate a parent which was apparently working. Terry kept glancing over. Charlie was next to his brother, looking at something on his cellphone.

The entire situation was surreal, Stacey thought. Whatever Terry's reason was for coming over here on Christmas, if he thought he had the upper hand, he was mistaken.

"Been a while since we saw you, Dad. So, how have things been?" Eric spoke up, slamming the legs of the chair hard against the floor.

Terry flinched and then his face turned to stone again, "We've been planning the wedding."

"Ah, the wedding. And what a wedding it'll be, right? Going to be beautiful," Eric said in a tone so dry that if Stacey didn't know him at all, she would have thought that he was serious.

"How is the planning going?" Charlie asked, jumping into the conversation.

"Fine," Terry said at the same time Adele said, "Stressful."

The brothers glanced at each other. Something passed between them. It was so quick that Stacey thought she might have imagined it. Eric leaned forward toward his dad.

"Stressful? Ah, that's no good. You should do what Stacey and Charlie did. The courthouse. Skip that mess."

"No, thank you. I would like a proper wedding," Adele replied primly.

"Well, what do I know, right?" Eric said and held up his hands in front of his chest. "I'm not getting married any time soon."

From the other side of the table, Kailyn laughed loudly, "Yet! You mean 'yet'!"

"Right," Eric swiftly corrected. "Yet. Who knows what could happen?"

Stacey cleared her throat. She was all for making their father squirm, but she wasn't going to give Kailyn any hope of Eric proposing. He must have sensed what she was thinking because he quickly changed the subject.

"Where are you guys going to get hitched? I mean, this is going to be a pretty big deal, right? Merging of the companies. Fantastic."

"It doesn't concern you, boy," Terry said, finding renewed vigor. "You won't be attending. I've been trying to get in touch with you for months and you have been off doing Lord knows what. I don't need you mucking up the wedding."

"I'm crushed, truly," Eric replied in a voice that sounded decidedly *not* crushed. "But what can I do?" He picked up a pastry and crammed the entire thing in his mouth as he shrugged at his father.

Terry looked disgusted and turned his attention to Charlie. "What about you, boy? You haven't been speaking to me either. Here I am, planning a wedding and you haven't offered to help."

"Been a little busy," Charlie replied lightly.

Terry scoffed, "With what? Not your business, I'm sure. I've been hearing things –"

"You've been hearing things because you're pulling the strings. That means you're all caught up so there's no need to talk about it. Let's just focus on the wedding. Must be exciting to remarry after all these years."

Terry stared at Charlie for a long moment. His eyes went to Eric who was still attempting to chew the pastry he had shoved into his mouth. Kailyn yawned loudly. Stacey turned to look at her.

"Are you tired?"

"Yeah, I didn't get much sleep last night, if you know what I mean," she said and laughed loudly.

Behind her, she heard Adele make a disapproving noise. Terry looked disgusted. Eric winked at Kailyn, who pursed her lips and blew a kiss back at him.

"Would you like to nap? Why don't I show you to one of the guest rooms?" Stacey offered, getting to her feet.

Kailyn agreed, to Stacey's relief. Yes, the woman was a mess, but Stacey felt strangely protective of her. She didn't deserve to be put on display just to piss off Terry. She got Kailyn into one of the guest rooms, who fell asleep almost the instant her head hit the pillow. Covering her with a blanket, Stacey went back into the dining room.

Adele launched into a story about searching for the perfect wedding dress. There was something monotone and mechanical to her story, as if she had been repeating it for days on end. Terry looked bored as he stared into his coffee cup. Stacey wished she could cut through the garbage and figure out why he was really here.

Eric, of course, was taking everything very seriously. He was pretending to be so fascinated by Adele's story that it was almost comical. He moved to the opposite side of the table and was leaning forward, nodding his head often.

Stacey sat down next to him and glanced over at her husband. He wasn't acting as over the top as his brother, but he was still actively nodding his head while Adele told her story.

"Anyway, so I get it back and the dress didn't fit. For the third time, if you can believe it," Adele was saying.

"No!" Eric exclaimed, "That's ridiculous."

Stacey shot him a look but he ignored her. Even so, up this close she could see that he was fighting the urge to laugh. Something caught her eye, however, on his collarbone. She hadn't noticed it before. The night before, he had worn a shirt with a collar that covered it. Not to mention, she had been preoccupied with helping him staunch the blood from his nose.

Without thinking, Stacey exclaimed, "Did you get a tattoo?"

Adele stopped speaking, looking annoyed at having been interrupted. Eric looked down at his collarbone and yanked his shirt down a little. There was a tattoo there – two very small birds circling around each other in blue ink. It was a simple tattoo and ultimately generic. She had no idea why he would have gotten it.

But the reaction from Terry was almost immediate. "A *tattoo*? This is what you do? You run off and get tattoos? Disgusting!"

"I think I was drunk," Eric replied with obvious glee at bothering Terry. "Am I grounded, Dad?"

"Disgusting. I can't believe I raised a son who's smoking and getting tattoos. Charlie, tell your brother. Tell him how disgusting that is."

Eric pulled out a pack of cigarettes. "Wow, speaking of cigarettes. Been about an hour since my last one." He stood up and looked over at Charlie. "Are you going to lecture me?"

But Charlie shook his head, "Nah, I could go for a smoke myself."

"What?!" Terry exclaimed, also getting to his feet. "Stop this! Your mother wouldn't approve of any of this."

But the brothers didn't reply. Charlie opened the balcony door, allowing Eric to step out first. Stacey watched them as he slid out a cigarette and handed one to Charlie. Then he pulled out his lighter and leaned over, lighting up the cigarette. Terry watched as Charlie took a drag from it. Then Eric lit his up and did the same. The two of them then turned their backs on Terry as they smoked.

Terry turned toward Stacey. She braced herself for a lecture – how could she do this, what did she do to his boys – but instead he asked for more coffee.

Surprised, Stacey nodded and took the empty carafe into the kitchen to refill it. As she was doing so, Adele came into the kitchen, eying Stacey warily.

"Need something?" she asked Adele.

"How did you get them to get along?"

"What?"

"Eric and Charlie. It's clear what they're doing. Trying to show Terry he has no power over them anymore. I'm assuming that it's your doing."

Stacey poured the carafe full of coffee and then replied, "I can't force those things. Whatever happened, it was ultimately up to them."

Adele marched over and yanked the coffee away from Stacey. She turned to look at her yet didn't feel afraid. She used to feel insecure when it came to Adele. Here was a woman that Terry wanted in the family. He had wanted her to marry Charlie and help control the company. But Stacey had been allowing Adele to have that power.

Staring at Adele now, she felt only pity. This person who wanted nothing more than to marry into this family at any cost. Why did Stacey feel so insecure around her?

"He's going to call off the wedding. He hasn't said it yet. But I can feel it. I'm going to lose everything I have spent planning," Adele said to her in a thin voice.

"I'm sorry," Stacey said, and then corrected herself. "No. Not really. But I am sorry that you think this is the only way to live your life. Because you're pretty and rich and bored. So, you've made getting into this family your entire life goal. And I'm sorry for that, because you are wasting real talents."

Adele looked as if she had been smacked in the face before replying, "You're the one who ruined it. Charlie would have married me. I was so close and then you swept in with your sob story about being poor. He ate it up."

"I'm not interested in discussing me or whatever you think of me, Adele. Terry is here because he doesn't want to marry you, right? This whole thing is some Christmas guilt trip in disguise. He thought Charlie would come back when he said he was going to marry you and now he realizes that isn't the case."

"Yes. Yes, okay, you're right. Is that what you want me to say? You seem to forget that I have known this family a lot longer than you have, Stacey. I know what Terry is like. There isn't a kind bone left in his body. He needs Charlie's leadership. He keeps trying to bribe people not to work with Charlie or to not leave the company to go work for Charlie. But the truth is that his son has a strong following there. They respect him as a leader and they hate that he left."

"You mean…"

"Yes," Adele said quickly, "I mean that Terry is bleeding money trying to bribe people to stay. Most of the people who work higher up want to jump ship and help Charlie out with this new company. And instead of just stopping this madness, Terry has come here in one final attempt to bring Charlie back."

"It won't work," Stacey said simply. "Charlie has put too much into this. He knows what his father is doing and just refuses to go back to him. Terry can marry you, he can bleed himself dry in bribing people to stay but time will tell."

"Eric and Charlie are getting along," Adele said. "At least for now. Terry wasn't expecting that. He never wants them to get along. Surely, you've noticed that by now. Easier to keep them separated than friendly. If they get along now…"

"Tell Terry it's over. It's over for you too, Adele. Get a hobby or something. Go travel. I don't know. Just don't waste time on this anymore."

She gently took the coffee out of Adele's hands and went out to the dining room. Terry watched the brothers out on the balcony. Eric was lighting up a second cigarette. Charlie, who was only smoking to irritate his father, took a slow, deep drag. Stacey poured a cup of coffee for Terry, who turned to look at her.

"Would you like a pastry?" Stacey offered.

"Where is Adele?"

"In the kitchen."

He made a clucking noise and then looked down at his coffee, "Is there any sugar in this place?"

"Sugar, coming right up," Stacey said politely and slid the sugar bowl from the other end of the table over to him.

Terry eyed her warily as she sat back down. He scooped two spoonsful of sugar into the mug as Stacey grabbed a pastry. She took a bite of it and smiled at Terry.

"You're an interesting woman," he finally said to her.

"Is that right?"

"At first, I thought all of this was your fault. That you were some poor girl looking for hand-outs. I heard about your sister marrying Jacob. No one could love that boy."

"He's quite nice."

"He's a dullard," Terry retorted.

"Still nice," Stacey smiled.

There was a beat of silence before Terry went on, "But I can see now you aren't going anywhere. Charlie is quite taken with you. Eric seems to be fond of you too."

She remained silent. It almost felt as if Terry was fishing for something and she wasn't going to give him any information. She wasn't stupid enough to mention that Eric kissed her all those months ago.

When she didn't reply, Terry said, "You should tell Charlie. Tell him that the company is for him. His mother wouldn't want him to throw this out the window. This investment firm – it's foolish. What sort of billionaire walks away from a company he was in charge of to start an investment firm?"

To get away from you. To make it on his own and not be in your shadow. But instead, Stacey nibbled on the pastry in silence.

Terry seemed almost unnerved by the fact she wasn't speaking because he continued on. "It's funny seeing the two of them getting along. They were always against each other, you know. It didn't help that Eric always chased after Charlie's girlfriends. I'm sure it is just a matter of time until he throws himself at you. What will you do then, I wonder? Most people find Eric very alluring even though he isn't as good-looking as Charlie. Do you know why that is?"

Stacey took another bite of the pastry. She could see Charlie lean over to tell Eric something who glanced over at the dining room table. She gave him a small wave and he grinned before turning back to Charlie.

"Are you listening to me? Do you hear me?" Terry was bothered now. "I'm trying to warn you about Eric."

"Eric is fine," Stacey replied. "The only reason he has any issues, I believe, is because of you. Would your wife really be okay with you telling her sons that one of them is worthless? Would she be okay with you trying to ruin a business your other son is starting? I never met their mother but if she was anything like her sons, I doubt that she would think kindly of you. Now, if you will excuse me…"

She stood up and grabbed her hoodie that was tossed on the counter. Terry stared at her with an expression that could only be described as shock. Adele came into the dining room just then, carrying a Bloody Mary. Stacey made her way to the balcony and slid the door shut behind her.

Charlie was laughing at something Eric had said. His head was thrown back and he was laughing loudly. It wasn't a phony laugh to get Terry's attention either. It was genuine.

"Everything okay out here?" Stacey asked.

Charlie pulled her in close to him and kissed the top of her head. "Yeah, Eric was just telling me about some bar fight he got into a month ago."

"Put your smoke out, idiot." Eric swiped the cigarette out of Charlie's mouth, butting it out along with his.

"Aw, you're cramping our Piss off Dad session," Charlie joked and kissed her – he tasted of smoke.

"Was he mad?" Eric asked. "When Charlie agreed to have one, I thought he was gonna have a stroke."

"Yeah, he doesn't understand why you two are getting along now. He's freaked."

"Those cigarettes taste disgusting. I have no idea how you can smoke them," Charlie said.

Eric shrugged. "Crippling addiction? I don't know. I hardly notice anymore."

"You should quit." When Eric shrugged, he kept on. "I'm serious. How are you going to be around our kid if you die of lung cancer?"

Surprise crossed Eric's face and he said uncertainly, "Figured I wouldn't be around the kid at all."

"Yeah, well," Charlie exhaled slowly, "wouldn't be fair to my kid, would it? They should see for themselves what a complete idiot their uncle is. It's high comedy."

Eric playfully punched Charlie in the arm but he was laughing. Stacey felt as if she had stepped through the looking glass into an alternate universe. She could practically feel Terry staring at them through it.

"Dad say anything?" Charlie asked her.

Stacey nodded and told the brothers what had unfolded between Adele and then Terry. They listened and both of them wore identical looks of focus on their faces. For the first time since she had been around the two of them, they actually looked related.

When they finished, Charlie spoke first. "So, he's cornered, basically. He needs me to come back."

"Fuck it. You better not cave now," Eric said gruffly.

"I'm not going to. But I don't want the entire company to go to shit because of me. Are you sure you won't take it over?"

"Positive. I thought I wanted that. But I just wanted it because Dad put the idea in my head. I don't want it now."

"Then I have an idea but it will depend on making Dad admit he's fucked up."

"Good luck," Eric snorted.

"No, I think you might have a chance now," Stacey replied. "He seemed sort of all over the place."

"Yeah, plus you just told him our dead mother would think he's an asshole," Eric pointed out and crossed his arms. "I'm pretty impressed."

Charlie looked at Stacey. "I'm going to go try to talk to him." He looked over at Eric. "Try not to murder Adele, or fuck Kailyn while I deal with Dad."

"Yeah, yeah. I'll be fine." Eric waved his hand.

Charlie kissed Stacey again before heading back inside the penthouse. She watched as he said something to Terry who then got to his feet and followed him out of the dining room. Adele was on her phone, texting away.

Stacey pulled her hoodie around her and exhaled nervously.

Chapter Ten

"So," Eric said as he turned to look over at the city, "I actually did want to talk to you."

"Well, if you're going to kiss me, I'd like to suggest holding off. I don't feel like cleaning up blood today."

He laughed and ran his fingers through his hair. "No, no kissing. I wanted to apologize for that. For obvious reasons. At the time, it made sense. You know, Dad said all that shit about me and it was easier to just become what he called me instead of fighting against it."

"That's what you've been doing these past few months, haven't you?"

"Yes. Basically just going from town to town, drinking and sleeping my way around. When I came here with Kailyn, it was just in a moment of ultimate self-destruction. I was hoping secretly that Charlie would beat the shit out of me for what I did."

"Pretty sure he did just that."

"No. We were both holding back. I think even then he didn't want to attack me. After Allison kicked me out like that, I thought to myself *what am I doing? Why did I really come back to the party?*"

Stacey shivered as a gust of wind kicked up over the balcony. Eric noticed and offered his jacket. She declined but he slid out of his jacket and handed it to her anyway.

"Come on. I'm not the pregnant one," he said.

She relented and slipped into the jacket, pulling it over her hoodie, asking, "So, why did you come back to the party?"

"I guess I wanted to see Charlie again. He is my brother, after all. And I was just going down this road of doing whatever I wanted and ultimately, I wanted to see him. I didn't realize it until after I left the party though. I was trying to figure out how to make things right when Dad showed up."

"Well, that's a big step from before when the two of you were content to fight every second. And that isn't just you. Charlie was quick to fight with you no matter what as well."

"I just wanted to apologize to you. For what I did. And I knew when I did it that it was wrong."

"Can I ask you something?" When he nodded, she said, "You said that you wanted to do it that night you were drunk, but you stopped yourself. What did you mean? Mess things up between Charlie and yourself?"

Eric looked surprised for a moment.

A thought struck her. "Eric – you don't… I mean, I assumed that you kissed me to get to Charlie, not because –"

He cut her off swiftly, "I'm over it. Whatever I was feeling at the time, it's gone now. It was stupid to begin with. It won't ever happen again. It shouldn't have happened in the first place. I just hope we can move on from it and you can forgive me for overstepping a serious line."

"Yeah. Yeah, I forgive you. Of course."

Eric visibly relaxed and nodded. "Great. And listen – thanks. For everything. I know you were pushing really hard for me and Charlie to make up. And I think we still have a lot to work through together, but I think this is an important start."

"Me too," Stacey said, and she meant it.

Eric smiled that slow grin that she had come to know well over the past year, and he said, "Remember when I introduced myself as Devin? That was one of my better ones."

She rolled her eyes. "Don't start. Remember when I slapped you?"

"You felt so bad about it too! I should have told you I'm used to being slapped regularly by women I piss off."

She laughed. That was when the sliding door opened and Charlie stepped out. His face was unreadable. Stacey could feel her heart skip a beat and she went over to him.

"How did it go?"

For a split second, she wondered if he was going back to the company. It would be a blow, Stacey decided, not only to her but to Eric, who was looking forward to having a brother again and moving on.

But then a smile broke out across Charlie's face and he smiled brightly, "I'm going to be merging my investment firm with Dad's company. He's relinquishing control. He would rather step down completely than see the company melt. He's calling off the wedding with Adele."

Stacey exclaimed in surprise as Eric said, "That was fast!"

"He crumbled almost right away. Stacey was right. He was nervous and on edge. I just had to give the little push."

Charlie was beaming now, and he brought Stacey in for a hug. His lips pressed against hers and she could feel the warmth from his body. It cut through the jacket and the hoodie she was wearing. She could feel his heart racing with excitement.

Eric came over and brought Charlie in for a hug. She couldn't recall ever seeing them hug before.

"So, what now?" he asked Charlie.

"Paperwork will be drawn up and we'll go from there. Going to be crazy busy for a while but it's always busy. We'll get things ready for the baby too."

Stacey smiled and then looked at Eric, "What about you? What are you going to do?"

"Take Kailyn home. Break up with her. Then, I don't know."

"You know, if you want to come help me out…" Charlie offered.

He shook his head. "Not yet. I need some air from the whole company. Might travel a bit. Properly travel this time, not just party. Figure out what the hell I'm doing."

"Well, if you decide that you want to be involved, let me know."

"Thanks," Eric said, and he smiled.

Stacey stared at the brothers with happiness filling her heart.

"So, is Dad leaving? Maybe we can enjoy this holiday after all," Eric said, playing with a cigarette, clearly trying to bury the urge to light it.

"He said he's going to stay for lunch and then leave with Adele."

"Man, when is he going to tell Adele the wedding is off? She's going to be pissed," Eric said.

As if in reply, Adele's voice rang out, "Are you fucking serious?"

Stacey widened her eyes. "I guess now. Man, your dad doesn't like to wait, does he?"

Charlie shook his head. "No, guess not. Although he could have easily waited until tomorrow."

"Look at the bright side," Eric offered.

"What? That Charlie is going to get his own company and merge it with his father's? I guess that is the bright side."

"No," Eric shook his head. "One less person to feed."

Charlie groaned and Stacey sighed. Eric grinned at them and then moved away to the other side of the balcony, waving his cigarette at them.

"Gotta quit those!" Charlie called after him.

He flipped off Charlie and Stacey watched him light the cigarette. The gesture was a teasing one, not serious. Stacey looked over at Charlie who was smiling and looking like he was on top of the world. How could he not be? Terry came here for one last guilt trip, but it was finally Charlie's time to shine. There was no more control over him.

Even as Adele was freaking out indoors, Stacey decided that this was going to be a good Christmas after all.

Epilogue

Stacey yawned and waited for the coffee machine to beep. She had been up most of the night and was feeling as if someone had smacked her across the head with a frying pan. Next to her, Charlie was rummaging around in the fridge.

"No Bloody Mary mix," he remarked.

"He'll have to get over it." Stacey yawned.

Charlie laughed at that. Jessica padded in and looked up at the two of them with wide brown eyes. "Bloody Mary mix?"

"Not as gross as it sounds," Charlie replied, scooping their daughter up in his arms.

"More gross, actually," Stacey joked.

There was the sound of rushing feet as Alex burst into the kitchen. He was about ten now, all long limbed and awkward looking. His glasses were slipping down the bridge of his nose and he was clutching a tablet in one hand.

"Wow, what's the rush?" Charlie asked him.

"The internet is down. Can I reset the router?"

"Sure, I guess, but it might just be down from the snow storm last night," Stacey said, but Alex was already taking off again like a shot.

She sighed and shook her head. Charlie laughed and looked at Jessica in his arms. "Your brother is silly."

The doorbell rang and Stacey glanced at the clock. "Can't be him already, can it?"

"Might be Allison."

"She said she'd come by later because of all the snow. I'll go see."

Stacey left the dining room and walked toward the front door. She opened the door and was surprised to see Allison and Jacob on the doorstep.

"Hey! I thought you'd come by later!"

"They plowed our streets early. It only took us like, an hour to get here," her sister joked. "You know, instead of the normal twenty. Merry Christmas!"

She threw her arms around Stacey. Allison, Jacob, and their son, Vinny, had been out of the country for the past three months. It was a surprise when they had come home a week ago. However, both women had been too busy to see each other.

"Get inside so you guys don't catch a chill or something. Vinny, how are you?" Stacey asked the seven-year-old.

"I'm okay. Mom got me this." He shoved something toward Stacey who looked at it.

"Looks cool," Stacey said, even though she didn't know what she was looking at.

"I'm gonna go show Alex," he said, and ran inside the house.

In the foyer, Allison explained, "It's a tablet that comes with games. That way he doesn't break Jacob's again. It's sturdier too, since he tends to throw them around."

Stacey recalled last Christmas when Vinny, in a burst of excited energy, accidentally knocked her cell phone off the counter and shattered the screen. Allison's son was like a hurricane in human form. He would sweep into rooms full of energy and didn't seem to ever run out. He was more like Allison than Jacob, although sometimes he would get very serious about things.

"Well, hopefully the house remains unscathed," Stacey remarked as they took off their coats.

Jacob lifted up a bag he was holding. "Gifts. Just put them under the tree?"

"Yeah, please. You guys want anything to drink?"

"Coffee," they said in unison.

As Jacob went over to the large Christmas tree and began to put their gifts under it, Allison looked around.

Alex was greeting Jacob, talking to him excitedly about computers or something that Stacey didn't understand.

"Kid is going to be a tech whiz," Allison remarked.

"He's already too smart for his own good," Stacey joked as they went into the kitchen.

"Maybe Vinny and Alex can team up. Create a brand new business or something. Imagine that."

"Seems a long time away."

"Maybe. But they're already growing up so fast. Before you know it, Jessica is going to be a teenager, driving you crazy."

"That's if I survive Alex. For some reason, I think he's going to be a handful. Not as much as Vinny though. Pretty amazing, your child is basically just like you. What goes around comes around."

"I was never that bad," Allison protested. "You just didn't like what I was doing. That's all."

"Yeah, yeah," Stacey began pouring her sister a cup of coffee. "So, you have a good trip?"

"Mostly, but it was just Jacob working on the expansion. I tried to keep Vinny in line and not have him cause an international incident."

"How did that go?"

"Couple of close calls but I think we made it through all right." She smiled.

"Things have been pretty quiet here."

"As quiet as things can be with Charlie. I saw his article in that magazine last month. I don't even remember the name of it. That fancy business one. Pretty impressive."

Stacey looked over at Charlie, who was now in the living room with Jacob and the kids. Vinny was showing Alex his new tablet. Jessica hovered behind Charlie and Jacob as if the business conversation they were having made complete and utter sense to her.

"Well, Charlie gets bored if he isn't working on new projects."

"Sort of like you."

Stacey shrugged, "Maybe a little."

"Come on, you're selling yourself short again –"

There was a sudden thud of something dropping, followed by Vinny saying, "Oops."

Stacey and Allison grabbed their coffees and went out to the living room. Vinny had knocked over a small statue that they brought back from China a couple years ago. Luckily, it wasn't broken. Stacey bent over and picked it up as her sister lectured her son.

"Sorry, I was showing Alex the photo mode on the tablet," Vinny replied.

"Just be more careful. I swear, you're all flying limbs," Allison said.

"Dad said he was like that when he was little," Vinny protested.

"Were you really?" Stacey asked, surprised. "I can't picture that."

Jacob looked sheepish. In the years he had been with Allison, the long endless conversations had faded as he became comfortable with silence. The nervous, social anxiety that had once compelled him to fill every moment with stories about himself had slowly tapered off, due to Allison's touch.

Even with the changes that had happened over the last few years, trying to imagine Jacob as a clumsy lanky ball of energy took everyone in the room by surprise.

"Always finding out something new," Allison finally said.

"I grew too fast. Had a hard time controlling my limbs," Jacob remarked primly.

"Does this mean I can't control my limbs?" Vinny inquired.

"You can control your limbs just fine," Alex chimed up. "Just look around once in a while."

Vinny looked as if he was thinking about this when Stacey's son turned to her and asked, "When is Uncle Eric getting here?"

"Soon. We won't open gifts until he gets here."

"I hope he likes what I got him."

"I'm sure he will."

He nodded and flopped onto the couch next to Jessica, who was holding onto her doll and making it talk in a high-pitched voice. Jacob turned back to Charlie, picking up where their conversation had left off. Allison glanced over at Stacey.

"Today is going to be a tiring day."

"Holidays always are."

"Worse for you. I've seen how Alex gets when Eric is around."

Stacey smothered a groan and shook her head. "He idolizes him though. At least he's not the same Eric he was when I met him. And I know Eric loves him too. We couldn't ask for a better uncle for our kids."

"Been a while since you saw him, right?"

"Three years," Stacey replied.

"And what has he been doing? Writing or something?"

She nodded. "Yup. Traveling the world and writing about it. I still can't imagine him writing. But he sort of floated around for those five years and then started putting everything to paper, remember?"

"Can't imagine Eric writing anything that people could relate to."

"It's been a long time since you saw him, though." Stacey pointed out.

It was true. The last time Eric came down to visit, Allison had been in Asia with Jacob. It had been easily about four or five years since her sister had seen Eric. She was still picturing the mess of a man that he was while everything unfolded with Terry. That was a far cry from who he was now.

Alex turned around on the couch, "When is he gonna get here?"

"Soon. Snow delays everything. Just be patient."

"Be patient," Jessica repeated next to him.

Alex rolled his eyes at his younger sister. Sensing a possible fight, Stacey clapped her hands together, "Let's get breakfast started. Who wants to help?"

Jessica hopped to her feet and hurried over. Stacey grabbed her hand. She knew Alex wasn't going to want to help with breakfast.

Allison, Jessica and Stacey got to work in the kitchen. As Stacey looked around at everyone, she felt happiness wash over her. It was nice having everyone home for the holidays.

"I want another chocolate Santa!" Vinny pleaded with Allison later on that day.

"No way. No more sugar. You're cut off."

Changing tactics, he turned to look at Jacob. "Dad, I want a chocolate Santa. Come on."

"You heard your mother. Let it go, Vinny."

Vinny pouted and plopped down on the couch, crossing his arms. He looked away from his parents.

Allison whispered, "He'll be asleep in moments."

Stacey stifled a laugh. There was a knock on the door. Before she could even move, Alex took off like an arrow, running toward the door. Stacey trailed after him. She could hear him exclaim in excitement and then heard the low timber of Eric's voice.

She paused in the foyer. Eric stood there, talking to Alex, who was beaming up at him. He was bouncing on the balls of his feet, telling Eric about some computer program. Eric caught sight of Stacey and looked up at her.

In the three years since she had seen Charlie's brother, he looked mostly unchanged. Eric had always looked older than he really was. Ten years ago, Stacey thought that had been a detriment. Now, however, he appeared to be almost frozen in time.

"New tattoo," she remarked.

His hand went to his neck where she could just make out the top of a tattoo. Alex was bobbing around at his feet.

"A new tattoo? Cool! Dad said I can't get any tattoos until I'm an adult. But I'm gonna get one like yours, Uncle Eric."

Eric put his hands gently on Alex's shoulders, steering him away from the front door. "Well, don't tell your dad that, okay? But you *can* go tell him that I'm here though?"

Alex nodded and took off again. Eric took off his jacket and hung it up. He turned to look at Stacey.

"You look good."

"Thanks. You look the same."

"You mean devilishly handsome? Thanks sis!" He gestured to his face as he took a step toward her.

"Well, you look good. Healthy, at least. Must be from all that traveling."

"Yeah, I've gotten in shape from all that climbing around. Although, I was just in Mexico. Didn't do anything there besides just sit by the beach."

"You as a writer. Who would have thought that would ever happen?" Stacey asked.

"Not me. Books have been selling well though. They want me to go on a book tour for my next one but…" He shrugged.

"You don't want to?"

"I don't know. Nervous, I guess. Seems weird to be surrounded by people wanting to talk about my books. Not used to the idea yet."

"Well, don't worry about it for today. Come on." She gestured for him to come into the living room.

Eric hesitated and asked, "Anyone here smoke?"

Puzzled, she replied, "No. Allison and Jacob are here. That's it. Why?"

He cleared his throat. "I quit three years ago but I still get really antsy around anyone who does."

Stacey's eyes widened and she said in disbelief, "You quit?"

"Don't get excited. You know I've tried it before."

That was true. Eric struggled on and off with quitting smoking. Sometimes he'd go months without touching one only to cave one night at a social event. He said he wanted to quit so he could be around as an uncle. Even so, it hadn't been easy. For him not to have a cigarette in three years was a Christmas miracle unto itself.

"Yeah, but three whole years! That's your longest time yet."

"Well, don't make a big deal out of it, alright? I still don't feel like it's going to stick."

"No one smokes here. Smoke free zone. Come on and say hi to Charlie."

The living room was empty. Jacob, Charlie and the children were in the family room at the back of the house. Allison stuck her head out of the kitchen.

"Eric. Great, you're here. I need you."

"Wow, wasn't expecting that turn of events. I know you haven't seen me in a while but…"

Allison rolled her eyes, "I can't open this jar, idiot."

Eric went into the kitchen to help her. The jar lid popped off and he opened the fridge.

"Don't bother. No Bloody Mary mix," Stacey casually warned.

"What? Seriously? Come on."

"We had a snow storm come through, in case you didn't notice. You're lucky that you're here at all," Stacey remarked.

"Man, what a let-down. Here I am for the entire week and I can't have a Bloody Mary."

"If you want some so badly, then you can go out into this weather and get some."

"Better not. Your son would want to go with me and I would probably lose him or something in the snow," Eric replied before turning to look at Allison. "Everything well with you?"

"Yeah, thanks. Just trying to keep Vinny under control."

Eric grabbed an energy drink out from the back of the fridge. Stacey couldn't recall ever buying any of those things. He always managed to find the weirdest stuff in their fridge.

Cracking it open, he said to Allison, "Can't believe you two are still married." When Allison glared at him, he added quickly, "Because you two were so different at the start of everything. And Jacob was so dull."

"He isn't anymore. He just needed support and some understanding," Allison replied. "And we love each other now. It just took time."

Eric shrugged. "Who am I to judge? I don't have any sort of family life going on."

"Can't imagine why," Allison quipped as she left the kitchen.

Stacey looked at him. "Still great at annoying people, I see."

"Come on, everyone thought they'd be divorced by now. But they've been together longer than most marriages these days. Besides you and Charlie, of course."

"Well, they're happy together. Like Allison said, just took some time. But things worked out. What about you, anyway? No girlfriend or anything?"

"Nah. I mean, there's been lots of women, don't get me wrong. But I'm not interested in settling down."

"Always going to be a bachelor?"

"Most likely."

"What's going on in here?"

Stacey turned around to see Charlie walking into the kitchen with a grin on his face. He went over to his brother and brought him in for a hug. Even now, after all these years, it was still such a strange sight to see the two of them hugging one another.

"Nothing much. Telling Stacey here that I don't have any girlfriends."

"I think everyone has given up on you getting married," Charlie replied.

Eric shrugged. "Ah, well… what can I say? They like you because they think you're a starving artist. Or they like you because they figured out you have a bunch of money."

"Not everyone is like that," Charlie replied.

"Well, for the time being…" He trailed off as if he didn't know what else to say.

Sensing the subject coming to a close, Stacey spoke up, "Eric hasn't smoked in three years."

"No shit. Are you serious?"

"It's not a big deal, come on. I wanna hear what you've been up to. Besides what you've told me, I mean, in short phone calls. You've been busy since Dad died."

Terry had died of cancer four years ago. The death left Charlie and Eric with mixed feelings. Stacey couldn't blame them. After Charlie merged his new company with his father's, Terry still sprung up once in a while to be a thorn in his side. He never completely gave either of his sons the respect they deserved.

The death plunged Eric into a deep depression, causing him to go to Africa for a full year before coming back to see them. He later said that it was because he still felt as if he never lived up to what his father wanted or fully forgave him for what he put him through.

Charlie handled his father's death by throwing himself into work. He worked on expanding the company worldwide in the years after Terry died. The construction company was booming. Not to mention he had his investment company on the side. Recently, he was debating getting involved in media as well.

When Eric said that Charlie was keeping busy, it wasn't an exaggeration. Everything that Charlie had held off doing because of Terry came into full focus after his death.

Stacey brought Terry up a few times. He was always kind to their children, although Charlie had him on a tight leash. Even so, there was never any sort of forgiveness on either side.

Stacey was sometimes concerned the brothers had issues stemming from Terry that they never came to terms with while he was alive. But when she said as much to Charlie, he brushed her off.

"Eric is grieving in his own way. So am I," he said and hadn't brought up his father since.

"Busy, yes. But things are starting to settle down now. I was thinking about traveling a little. I think the kids should see more of the world."

"What about you? You want to travel?" This was directed at Stacey.

She knew what Eric was asking – could she leave to go travel? The real estate company that she had started with William had turned into a success. He had opened a few more branches across the country, with Stacey firmly entrenched as his 'right-hand.' Brad still worked there as well, although Amanda had quit once the two of them broke up. She went back to school full-time and became a history teacher.

"William has been bothering me to take a vacation for a while now. He wouldn't have a problem with it. I wouldn't mind taking a break either."

"Working and taking care of two kids. I don't know how the both of you do it. I get exhausted after hiking. Imaging hiking and then taking care of some kid on top of it."

"That's why you're the favorite uncle. You appear with all the cool stuff now and then and Alex and Jessica love you for it."

"Speaking of Alex, I should find him before he freaks," Eric said and headed toward the family room.

The two of them watched him leave and Stacey turned to look at Charlie. "So?"

"So, what?"

"You gonna ask him?"

"I don't know. I don't think he wants to take control of any branch office overseas. I know we thought maybe he would but seeing him now…"

"Yeah, I agree with you. I think he likes what he's doing. But I still think you should ask."

"Why?" Charlie looked puzzled.

"It'd be a good gesture. I think he'd like it. A formal invitation to work for you – ten years ago he never would have thought that would happen."

Charlie ran his fingers through his hair and watched as Eric was stalked over to Alex who began to show him something on his tablet.

"I'd like him to be around more."

"Never thought I'd hear you say that," Stacey said.

"Me neither," Charlie admitted. "But it's true. Sometimes I wish he would stay here a little longer."

"Well, we have the whole week with him. Think about asking him to stay for longer then."

She could tell Charlie was thinking about it. She grabbed some snacks and headed off toward the rest of the family.

<<◇>>

Later that night, once Jessica and Alex were safely in bed, they sat around the fireplace in the living room. Allison and Jacob left after Vinny fell asleep in his father's lap.

Eric was staring at the fire, holding a glass of whiskey as Stacey cleaned up some wrapping paper that was scattered around. Charlie was also drinking.

"Nah," Eric was saying. "I don't want to be in charge of an office. But the offer is appreciated. Thank you for thinking of me."

Stacey wasn't surprised. Eric had seemed against any kind of office job ever since Terry told him off that night.

Charlie, however, still looked a little crestfallen. "Well, I think you'd be perfect for it."

"Probably," he replied, cocky as ever, "but it just isn't my thing."

Charlie glanced at Stacey who nodded at him to keep going. He looked vulnerable, which was an expression she rarely saw on him.

"What could I do to convince you to stay around longer?"

Eric looked taken aback by this and blinked. "Stay around where? Here? The city?"

"That's right."

"Why would I stick around here?"

Charlie seemed to falter again. In the progress they had made over the years, coming right out and saying he wanted to spend more time around his own brother felt to be the biggest task yet.

He cleared his throat. "I think it'd be good for Alex if you were around. He's taken to you. Jessica likes you too. And with Terry gone, we don't have a lot of family left. I think it'd be good for the kids to be around their uncle."

Eric took a sip from his glass and glanced at Stacey. "What about you?"

"What?"

"You think I should be around your kids more?"

"They do really like you… for some reason," Stacey teased.

He looked back at Charlie and then grinned. It was the same grin from all those years ago when he knew he had someone where he wanted them.

"You miss me, huh, bro?"

Charlie groaned.

But Eric didn't stop. "You do! You really do. You miss your little brother. I don't blame you. I've been traveling the world a long time now, making my own way. No one has been around to drive you crazy like me. I'm flattered, really."

"Come on, would you stop?" Charlie protested but he was smiling.

"I suppose I could work on my next book here in the city. Might help me focus. Or completely ruin my focus in which I will then blame you."

"Fine, blame me. But you'll stay?"

Eric leaned back in the couch. "Yeah. I'll stay."

A smile broke out across Charlie's face and Stacey felt a warmth spread out across her body. Never, in a thousand years, did she ever think that this could have happened. The mere idea of Charlie asking Eric to stick around for longer felt like something conjured up in a dream.

But it was reality. The brothers, torn asunder by whatever hold Terry had over them, were finally and completely reconciled again. Stacey had her husband and her two wonderful children. She had a job that she loved and family and friends she adored.

Standing behind them, she watched as Eric flipped on the TV. The two began to instantly bicker about what to watch. Eric wanted to watch sports. Charlie wanted to watch a movie.

She glanced out the window. It felt like a lifetime ago when Charlie announced Terry was allowing the company merger. It was the book end of a whirlwind year.

Who would have thought that so much could have happened so quickly? Looking back at it now, Stacey had very few regrets. She knew that somewhere, Tina was looking down at her and smiling.

Everything was finally just right.

-The End-

If you enjoyed this title, I would appreciate your leaving a review of the book. Good reviews encourage an author to write as well as help books to sell. Good reviews can be just a few short sentences describing what you liked about the book without having a spoiler. If you could spend 30 seconds writing a review, I would appreciate it: you can review this title right now at your favorite retailer.

Here is a preview of **another story** you may enjoy:

TRICIA REACHED for another blanket. "Are you cold?" she asked.

Rebecca's breath was raspy as she responded. As her lungs shut down due to ALS, or Amyotrophic Lateral Sclerosis, her ability to speak had started to decline. Muscle by muscle, ALS targeted the body and made it impossible for the individual to live a normal life. It had started a few years ago with Rebecca's legs. Now, her lung muscles were starting to freeze as well. Tricia winced as she thought about the future. If Rebecca chose to use machines to stay alive, her entire body would eventually stop working. At some point, her mind would remain functioning and she would be locked into her body.

Rebecca managed to squeeze out a feeble yes. Reaching over to the cupboard, Tricia removed a blanket and carefully tucked her in. Tricia had spent years training to be a nurse and really liked her job. Since she was an excellent nurse, she had caught the eye of the billionaire, John, at one of the couple's many trips to hospitals around the country. He had noticed the love and care she took with each patient. After a moment's hesitation, Tricia had allowed him to convince her to take care of his wife.

Pictures of Rebecca dotted the room. Since she was unable to leave, John had striven to make her room look like favorite memories of her life and activities. A young, healthy Rebecca smiled in each photo. In the few years she had been physically active, she had acquired awards for horseback riding, cooking and other projects. Now, though, this time of physical fitness had passed. Instead of dashing through the fields on her favorite horse, Rebecca spent her time in this room. She had taken her difficulties in stride and was truly brave in the face of all of these medical issues.

Finishing with the blanket, Rebecca started to say something. Leaning closer to hear her, Tricia finally pulled up a chair. "What do you need, Rebecca?" she queried.

Sighing, Rebecca whispered, "I need to talk to John. I have to tell him how I want to die."

Squeezing her hand, Tricia nodded. "Once I leave your room, I will go get him. Just in case he is not around, did you want me to give him a message?"

Rebecca tried to nod, but her head did not respond all the way. "Yes, I do. You need to tell him that I do not want any machines. He could keep me alive forever with a breathing tube, but I do not want to live a life where I am permanently locked into my body. And," she paused and struggled to take another breath. "I do not want him to stop enjoying life or waiting around for my eventual death. If God wants to take my soul now, we should not interfere."

Tricia nodded sadly. Most patients with ALS were more afraid of being stuck within their minds than actual death. She understood, but she could not imagine what life would be like without Rebecca's gentle soul. "I will tell him," she said.

Leaving the room, Tricia traversed the hallways of the mansion. John had built his fortune by buying and selling real estate properties. His initial money had arrived through an early investment in the dot com boom before the bubble burst. After seeing the dangers of the stock market, he had started to just buy and rent out properties. Even with the recent recession, he still made a profit. Instead of selling his properties or developing, he had continued to rent them out. In a decade or two, he had talked of selling and retiring. His plans had arrived before his wife had been diagnosed with ALS. Unwilling to speak of his life after her future death, Tricia had not asked about any change in his future plans.

The halls of the house were dotted with white oak doorways that led to a myriad of rooms. Plush white carpet softly surrounded Tricia's feet as she walked. She dreaded the conversation that was about to happen. Every day, she updated John about the status of his wife. Unfortunately, she seldom had good news to share. She nodded to John's secretary as she entered the office. Unlike most rich men, he used a male secretary. Before talking had become so difficult, Rebecca had explained that he tried to hire primarily males so that Rebecca would never worry about his fidelity. Since Tricia was intended to cater just to his wife, she had been allowed to work there despite her gender.

If you enjoyed this sample then look for **Love Anew: Lonely Billionaire Romance Series, Book 1**.

Here is a preview of **another story** you may enjoy:

Suspicion: Elusive Billionaire Romance Series, Book 1

"**I WANT** to know who the hell is responsible for this mess!" boomed Hendrick from the front of the boardroom.

Silence filled the room as all the top people in the company stared at Hendrick in awe. They knew he wasn't the kind of guy to be messed with. Considering the company had just been charged with federal and criminal charges for dumping industrial waste into the Arctic Ocean, they knew it was best to stay silent.

"I return from vacation to find the prosecutor in my office to tell me that a company that I built from the ground up to help humanity is being accused of filling the ocean with waste! Waste??" He screamed across the table, his face turning an angry red. Hendrick stopped for a moment to compose himself and looked at each person at the table, assessing their worth.

"Pray it was not one of you frontrunners that made the decision to handle the waste of the company in this manner. Now go, and I expect reports hourly about how we are making this right and where waste should be going from now on."

Everyone got up from the table quickly and filtered out of the room. Hendrick watched them all leave and turned to his right-hand man, Geoffrey, the CEO of the company.

"Tell me you didn't know."

A broad-shouldered man, Geoffrey held an imposing frame that fit well with the red beard that made him appear like a Viking. He was incredibly loyal and a great asset to the company.

"You have known me your whole life Hendrick, I'm sure you know I had nothing to do with dumping waste into the ocean. The person in charge of a decision like that is one of your minions."

"How is it that the owner and CEO of a company had no idea that his own company has been poisoning the ocean?"

"Someone down the line obviously felt it would save the company a lot of money."

Hendrick snorted, "Ya and no one would ever find out that the Arctic Ocean was suddenly polluted? My god they have vessel numbers and everything, it was our guys to be sure, so how do I not know about it?"

"The prosecutors are doing their investigation and so are we. I can guarantee that we will find out who is responsible before anyone else does."

"I'm being prosecuted, Geoffrey! They think I knew about this madness."

"Look you didn't know and they can't prove that you did. You will have your day in court and they will simply have to let it go. They can't pull evidence from thin air so you're safe."

Hendrick went to the side table by the grand picture window. He poured them both a glass of bourbon, handing one to Geoffrey.

"I built this company because I believed in a vision and now our reputation is being smeared. All the while I'm off doing fundraisers and charity events while some asshole is destroying the ocean under my name."

If you enjoyed this sample then look for **Suspicion: Elusive Billionaire Romance Series, Book 1**.

Other Books by Shyla Starr

- Tenacious Billionaire BWWM Romance Series

- Elusive Billionaire Romance Series

- Lonely Billionaire Romance Series

- Ardent Billionaire Romance Series

- Fervent Billionaire BWWM Romance Series

- Audacious Billionaire BWWM Romance Series

Get the latest update on new releases from the author at:

https://shylastarr.com/newsletter/

About the Author - Shyla Starr

Shyla currently specializes in writing interracial romance stories and is a huge fan of the alpha male. Simply put, there just aren't enough stories about mixed couple romances, which is something she is aiming to fix.

Being a bookworm all her life, when Shyla discovered men she also realized how easy it was to fulfill her fantasies through her writing.

When not writing and fantasizing about men, Shyla enjoys dancing, reading and chilling with her friends.

Connect with Shyla Starr

I really appreciate you reading my book! Here are my social media coordinates:

Friend me on Facebook: https://www.facebook.com/shylastarrauthor

Follow me on Twitter: https://twitter.com/shylstarr

Check me out on Goodreads: https://www.goodreads.com/author/show/8436084.Shyla_Starr

Subscribe to my newsletter: https://shylastarr.com/newsletter/

Visit my website: https://shylastarr.com/

www.ingramcontent.com/pod-product-compliance
Lightning Source LLC
Chambersburg PA
CBHW021200110726
47900CB00002B/666